Road to Tater Hill

OTHER YEARLING BOOKS YOU WILL ENJOY

CAROLINA HARMONY
Marilyn Taylor McDowell

A THOUSAND NEVER EVERS
Shana Burg

HATTIE BIG SKY
Kirby Larson

GONE FROM THESE WOODS
Donny Bailey Seagraves

LIZZIE BRIGHT AND THE BUCKMINSTER BOY
Gary D. Schmidt

Road to Tater Hill

Edith M. Hemingway

A YEARLING BOOK

All rights reserved. Published in the United States by Yearling, an imprint of Random House Children's Books, a division of Random House, Inc., New York. Originally published in hardcover in the United States by Delacorte Press, an imprint of Random House Children's Books, a division of Random House, Inc., New York, in 2009.

Yearling and the jumping horse design are registered trademarks of Random House, Inc.

Visit us on the Web! www.randomhouse.com/kids

Educators and librarians, for a variety of teaching tools, visit us at www.randomhouse.com/teachers

The Library of Congress has cataloged the hardcover edition of this work as follows:
Hemingway, Edith Morris.
Road to Tater Hill / Edith M. Hemingway.
p. cm.
Summary: At her grandparents' North Carolina mountain home during the summer of 1963, grief-stricken after the death of her newborn sister and isolated by her mother's deepening depression, eleven-year-old Annie Winters finds comfort holding an oblong stone she calls her rock baby and befriends a reclusive mountain woman with a devastating secret.
ISBN 978-0-385-73677-0 (hardcover) — ISBN 978-0-385-90627-2 (lib. bdg.) — ISBN 978-0-375-89371-1 (ebook)
[1. Grief—Fiction. 2. Friendship—Fiction. 3. Depression, Mental—Fiction. 4. Parent and child—Fiction. 5. Grandparents—Fiction. 6. Mountain life—North Carolina—Fiction. 7. North Carolina—History—20th century—Fiction.] I. Title.
PZ7.H37743Ro 2009
[Fic]—dc22
2008024906

ISBN 978-0-375-84544-4 (pbk.)

Printed in the United States of America

10 9 8 7 6 5 4 3 2 1

First Yearling Edition

For my parents,
Frank and Mary Morris,
And
In memory of
my baby sister, Mary Kate

Road to Tater Hill

Chapter One

For months I had wished and wished the baby would be a girl, a little sister. Maybe I shouldn't have wished so hard. *A boy might have lived.*

Weren't wishes kind of like prayers? Maybe my wishing really did make things worse. I knew that didn't make sense, but nothing in this whole terrible day made sense.

Grandma closed the front door with a bang, as if announcing the end of a chapter in a book about our lives. "What a day," she said, dropping her purse to the floor. "I'm going to lie down. You should take a nap, too,

Annie. None of us got much sleep last night." Grandma headed to her room, not waiting for an answer.

A nap? I was almost eleven. I hadn't taken a nap for as long as I could remember. Besides, how could a nap change the way we all felt? We'd still wake up. It would all still be the same.

"She means well, Annie," Grandpa said. "We're all worn out." He looked like he wanted to say something more. I waited. Grandpa had grown older, just in this one day. His glasses were smudged, and his mouth and shoulders sagged. Gray stubble covered his chin.

"I thought . . ." Grandpa reached out to smooth my hair. "We all thought it would be okay this time." Another pause as he started down the basement stairs to his workshop. "She had red hair, you know. Very much like yours. A downy, reddish cap."

My baby sister had red hair like mine. If only I could have seen her, just once.

The house was silent. I walked from room to room with that heavy, tired feeling you have after you've cried for a long time. I looked out the windows. How could the sun still shine like it was just any normal day? The kitchen clock showed that it was only 2:45. Maybe I'd go down to the Millers'. If the Miller kids didn't know about the baby, I could *pretend* things were normal.

The walk down the winding dirt road to the Millers' farm seemed longer than ever before. Maybe it was because I usually ran down and didn't even notice passing

Loggers Hollow Church with its small fenced-in grave-yard. But this time that little graveyard was all I could think about. *I won't look, I won't look,* I repeated over and over to myself, but it didn't keep the vision of gravestones out of my mind. Soon my little sister would have a grave-stone of her own with her short, one-day life carved into it. Born July 13, 1963. Died July 14, 1963. Grandpa had buried her there earlier this morning—all by himself while Grandma and I stayed with Mama at the hospital.

"Aren't we having a funeral?" I had asked.

Grandma was quick to shush me. "We're trying to make it easier for your mama. Less for her to go through," she whispered, while Mama lay in bed with her eyes closed, looking like she was asleep. But I could see tears slipping through the cracks and sliding over Mama's face, soaking the pillow beneath her head. Grandma patted her hand, and I tried squeezing Mama's other hand, but she didn't squeeze back.

Easier? Nothing could make things easier right now—except if I were miles and miles across the ocean in Germany with Daddy, who didn't even know anything was wrong. This was probably something I should write down in the journal Daddy had given me before he left. Something I should tell him about my summer, but I didn't know if I could ever write this feeling down on paper.

After another curve in the road, the Millers' brick farmhouse was in sight, and the yard was spilling over with grandchildren. They lived in their own houses nearby, but today was Sunday. I knew they were all there for the big Sunday dinner old Mrs. Miller always cooked with the help of the four younger Mrs. Millers. If it wasn't raining, they set up long tables in the yard under the shade tree and carried out platters of ham and biscuits, cole slaw, sliced tomatoes, corn on the cob—more food than even all those people could eat. And there would be a fluffy coconut cake that Bobby's mother, the young Mrs. Miller with black hair, liked to bake. After I scraped those tiny flakes of coconut off the frosting, it sure tasted good.

Whichever Mrs. Miller was closest would always set one more plate for me if I was around. I slipped in like I belonged there, just another member of their overflowing family, from crawling babies all the way up to the three older teenagers, who weren't around so much now. The only not-so-good parts were old Mr. Miller spitting his brown tobacco juice on the ground—once right next to my foot—and all the buzzing flies that flew straight from the cows in the meadow to the food on our plates.

By now their Sunday dinner would be over, but it looked like all the kids were playing dodgeball, including Bobby. He was twelve and only a year older than me— kind of like the big brother I never had. His curly black hair, just like his mama's, stood out above the heads of all his cousins and younger brothers and sister. Why couldn't I have all those brothers and sisters? At least a few cousins or . . . just one sister. Someone to have fun with, but also to have around during sad times like this. Someone to share this emptiness.

By the time I reached them, I could tell the kids already knew about the baby by the way they didn't look me straight in the face—even Bobby. The same way I couldn't quite look into Mama's eyes when I first walked into the hospital room that morning. They had stopped playing ball and stood in the driveway, kicking stones around in the dirt.

Finally Caroline, Bobby's nine-year-old cousin, asked, "Did you get to see the baby?"

I shook my head, not trusting my voice.

Silence stretched on until Bobby's little sister, Ruthie, asked, "What was her name?"

It took a few seconds before I could get the words out. "Mary Kate." *There*. I'd said it out loud, but my voice shook and I could feel my face turning red, the way it always did when I was about to cry. Why had I come down here? What was I supposed to say? This was worse than staying in the house.

Bobby cleared his throat and said, "Let's go swing on the rope. It's the last day the barn'll be empty. Papaw said we're making hay tomorrow."

My breath whooshed out. I hadn't even realized I was holding it, but now moving and breathing made me feel better, thanks to Bobby.

We all ran to the barn and one by one climbed up the ladder to the loft. Usually I had to wait for my turn, but

Bobby took the rope from its hook and announced, "Annie gets to go first." He handed it to me.

There was no time to gather the courage for that first step off the wood ledge. I gripped the rope before I could think about it, sucked in my breath as if I were jumping into the deep end of a swimming pool, and plunged down. For a second my legs thrashed around in the air until I managed to settle myself on the big knot, and I swept across the wide open space of the barn and up again to the other side. With one hand, I reached out to touch the far wall before swinging back to the loft. Bobby pushed me again, and I flew like a bird soaring across a field. Not a hawk or an eagle—more like a barn swallow that swooped through the sky, one so light nothing heavy or sad could pull me down to earth. I knew the other kids were waiting for a turn, but I pretended I didn't see them. If I kept on swinging, I wouldn't have to think.

A bulky shadow appeared in the square of bright light that was the open barn door. It was old Mr. Miller talking to Caroline. Then he left.

Caroline hollered up, "Papaw said we're walking up the road to pay our respects to Annie's family."

I didn't say anything, but held on tight to the rope as it slowed. The Miller grandchildren filed down the ladder and out of the barn—all except for Bobby. My barn swallow spell was broken. Now I was the pendulum on the grandfather clock, swinging back and forth until I wound down to nothing.

Caroline returned to the door. "Annie, aren't you coming?" she called.

Bobby turned to me. "You don't have to, you know." It was the first time he had looked straight into my eyes, and I was grateful he didn't say anything more.

Then he looked at Caroline. "Come on," he said, and they both left.

There was no point in staying in the barn all by myself. I slid off the rope. My feet hit the floor with a thud.

Outside, I squinted into bright sunshine. Old Mrs. Miller carried a covered casserole dish with two big hot pads. Bobby's mother carried a pie. Then came old Mr. Miller with Eddie, the youngest grandchild, on his shoulders. Ignoring Caroline, I walked next to Bobby in the long line of kids. He wouldn't try to talk to me if I didn't want him to.

I concentrated on avoiding rocks and not kicking up dirt along the road so I wouldn't have to listen to the hushed conversation. The church and the entrance to the graveyard were coming up, but I was determined to keep walking past without looking. Everyone slowed down and finally stopped. *What do they expect me to do?* I stared down at my feet until Ruthie asked, "Is that the baby's grave by the gate?"

I could not keep from turning. There it was–the tiny grave of Mary Kate. No more than a little pile of red dirt tucked away from the other graves, not far from the gate sagging from its hinges. A loud sob broke the silence.

Everyone turned to stare at me, and I realized I had made the noise.

Old Mrs. Miller handed the casserole dish to Bobby and reached toward me. For an instant I wanted Mrs. Miller's arms around me. But no, not with everyone watching. I couldn't just stand there and cry in front of them.

Without looking back, I took off running. It was harder in my loafers than in my usual sneakers. They were pinching my toes and heels, but there was no stopping now or even slowing down as long as the Millers were still in sight. My breath was coming in fast sobs by the time I passed the driveway to Grandma and Grandpa's house. *Harder, harder,* I pushed myself. Sharp pain stabbed my side. But I wasn't crying. As long as I was running, I didn't have to think about Mary Kate—only about reaching that first curve in the road. I hadn't run this fast since last spring at the fifth-grade field-day races.

The road never seemed so steep riding in the car. By now I was out of sight of the Millers, but I wouldn't stop until I passed the thick patch of blackberry bushes and rounded the second hairpin curve. My feet slowed to a stumbling run and finally to a walk. I circled back and forth across the road, the way I had seen runners pace at the end of a race.

My throat ached; my nose dripped. Worst of all, I was going to throw up all that greasy fried chicken I had forced down at that little diner in town on our way home from the hospital. Why did Grandma always think we had to eat a big dinner on Sunday, instead of a regular lunch? *Deep breaths. Deep breaths.* It was getting better. Maybe I wouldn't throw up.

I stopped walking and bent almost double, my long hair sweeping across the dusty road. This helped; I could breathe now, even think. But I didn't want to. With my eyes closed, I still saw the small mound of red clay. And the eyes. I could see the sad eyes of all the Millers watching me. Usually I liked being in the midst of their big family, but this time was different.

Shaking that picture from my mind, I looked straight down at my feet. The new white loafers I had been saving for school were coated with red dirt from the road.

"Oh no! Mama will *kill* me." I'd have to do something about my shoes before I went back to the house. Then I realized I was still wearing my dress. It wasn't like Grandma to let me go outside without changing when we got home, but of course Grandma had gone straight off to bed. None of the kids had said a word about the dress even when I was swinging on the rope in the barn. *Nothing is right anymore.*

Half expecting all the Miller grandchildren to appear around that last curve, I looked for a place to hide. Across the road, I pushed through a tangled clump of daisies and slip-slided down the stony bank toward the creek. There was no path here, but I knew I was getting closer as the gurgling grew louder. *Water.* A long drink—that was what

I wanted more than anything once I reached the rushing creek. But Mama had always told me never to drink the water from a river or stream. Even if it looked clear, it wasn't clean.

Plopping down on a flat boulder at the edge of the bank, I scooped up water and splashed it on my face. It was almost as good as taking a sip. I lifted my hair and ran my wet hand across the back of my neck. Then I took my shoes and socks off and inched my feet into the icy water, holding them there until they tingled up to my ankles and I could stand the cold no longer. When I pulled them out, my feet looked like I wore pale pink socks. That made me think about my white loafers again, and I knew I had to do something to fix them.

I dipped one sock into the water, wrung it out, and used it to wipe my shoes. It only made matters worse. Now they were streaked with red mud, and the white areas weren't white, but a dingy pink. I rubbed harder. The more I wiped, the worse they looked. *What am I going to do?* I rolled onto my stomach, leaned out over the edge, and dunked both shoes into the water. The current washed over them, but I could see, no matter what I did, that my shoes were ruined. *Nothing will ever be right again.* One finger at a time, I released my grip. The shoes bobbed and swirled away, one after the other. I watched them until they were out of sight. With or without shoes I'd be in trouble, but today it didn't seem to matter.

Sunlight sparkled through the trees and made lacy

shadows on the rock. I stretched out on my back on the warm hard surface, listening to the rushing of the water and looking up at the sky through the leafy ceiling above me. It reminded me of the crocheted canopy over my bed at home, and a wave of homesickness swept over me. I wished I were home in Florida with Mama and Daddy—the three of us together, looking forward to the baby—just like it had been a month ago. But . . . maybe I shouldn't be *wishing* again.

The air force was always moving Daddy around somewhere, but why to Germany and why now when we couldn't go with him? And why for two whole months? Before leaving, Daddy had driven Mama and me up here to North Carolina to stay with Grandma and Grandpa. Our trip started out like all our trips, with Daddy singing "Off we go into the wild blue yonder. . . ." I liked the song because it made our travels more exciting, and I did love the North Carolina mountains. Grandma and Grandpa's house in the mountains was more like home than any of the air force bases we had lived on. I had spent every summer here since I was two years old. This year Mama was sewing baby clothes, and I was wishing for a little sister. But everything went wrong. Mary Kate was born too early. *She might have lived if we'd been back in Florida. She might have lived if Daddy had been here.*

The lump was back, clogging my throat. I tried to swallow it and closed my eyes against more tears. *Not again.*

Scrambling to my feet, I scooped up a handful of

stones along the creek bank and hurled them into the water. Then I reached for more—little pebbles, big stones—anything my fingers could claw from the ground and fling into the creek. Harder. Faster. The more I threw, the more the lump melted. I dug deeper into the grainy dirt. My fingertips scraped against sharp rocks and slivers of shiny mica buried beneath the surface. Mud caked under my fingernails.

Working my hands around a bigger rock, I pulled and dug, pulled and dug some more. I was down on my knees now, using a stick to dig it out. Finally I pried it from the earth. It was heavier than any of the others, and I was ready to heave it into the creek. But something about this one made me stop. Something about *this* smooth river rock made me want to keep hold—to press it against the emptiness inside me. I ran my hand over it, then rinsed it in the rushing water and patted it dry with the skirt of my dress.

I stood with the rock balanced in both hands. How many thousands of years had the water and soil and other rocks been pounding this one out to its perfect oblong shape? It was about the size of one of Grandma's loaves of homemade bread, only heavier—just the right weight for a newborn baby. I nestled it into the corner of my arm, the way I would have cradled Mary Kate. Not like a doll; I was too old for dolls. But when I closed my eyes and imagined that the rock was a baby, there was something about the weight and feel of it that filled the empty hole inside me. I held it close for a long time while the water rushed past, birds chattered in the branches above, and a bee buzzed its way around the clusters of touch-me-nots.

Somewhere through the sound of the water and the thoughts in my head, I heard my name being called. *"Aaanneee, ohhh, Aaanneee."* The voice was drawn out long and on high notes, like an opera singer's. I knew it was Grandma. She and Mama always called me like that. It was embarrassing because the Miller kids started copying them in the same high voice. Grandma said the high notes made the sound carry better than regular yelling, but I thought both Grandma and Mama knew they'd get me home faster that way because I couldn't stand it.

"Aaanneee, ohhh, Aaanneee." There it went again. I gritted my teeth and looked around for a spot to hide my rock baby—somewhere I'd remember, so I could come back to hold it again. There was a V in the middle of a double tree—kind of like twin trees with shaggy bark peeling off. I placed the rock baby in the cradle of the V, then looked around to check landmarks.

The tree stood not far from the creek bank, just to the right of the big flat rock I had been sitting on. A rhododendron bush grew behind the tree. I was sure I could find it with its long, shiny leaves and puffy white blossoms.

"Ohhh, Aaanneee, wwwherre are you?"

Why can't Grandma just stop calling? My dress was wrinkled and damp with a big streak of mud on the skirt. There was nothing I could do about that now. I stuffed my socks in my pocket. Maybe I should have thought longer before dropping my ruined shoes in the creek.

Stepping on spongy moss when I could and avoiding the sharper rocks, I picked my way back until a motion at the corner of my eye caught my attention. Who was that farther over in the woods? It looked like a girl, but who would be walking around in the woods alone? The flickering sunlight and shadows made it hard to focus. Maybe the person was a small woman, not a girl. She used a walking stick and wore a long dress and a floppy old-lady sunbonnet on her head.

Ignoring yet another of Grandma's calls, I kept watching. The woman didn't turn her head, but continued up the steep hill crouched a little lower, as if she didn't want anyone to see her.

If I hadn't been barefoot, I would have followed at a distance. Grandpa always said I'd make a good scientist or detective because I liked to investigate. I stared at the disappearing figure until the woman blended in with the trees and bushes and shifting shadows. I wondered if I had really seen anyone at all.

Chapter Two

Both Grandma and Grandpa were standing on the porch watching for me when I reached the house. Grandma took one look at my bare feet and said, "Oh, Annie, what have you done with your shoes? And just look at your dress."

I hate having Grandma mad at me. It's not that she's so angry now, but more that she's disappointed in me, and that's worse. Whenever she's disappointed, she gets a sad look on her face and her mouth actually turns down at the corners like a painted-on frown. Of course she was already sad today. I couldn't even look at her face. "I'm sorry," I mumbled, focusing on my muddy toes.

"Now, Katherine," Grandpa said to Grandma. He wrapped his arm around my shoulder and continued. "*Shoes* are replaceable."

"I know, I know," Grandma answered. Then she was quiet for a moment while she lifted my chin.

I had to look up, and I could see she was trying to smile. As much as any of us could smile today. "It's okay, dear," Grandma said. "Now supper's ready. Wash your hands and set the table, please."

We didn't talk much at dinner, but I was surprised how hungry I was. We ate the chicken pot pie old Mrs. Miller had carried up the road and had a slice of the cherry pie Bobby's mother had made for dessert.

When we were finishing up, Grandma broke the silence. "I expect you know all the Millers were here this afternoon to pay their respects."

I nodded.

"Ruby Miller was worried about you, Annie. She said you ran off when they stopped by the church."

I nodded again.

"Oh, Annie." Grandma rubbed her forehead like she had a headache. "They meant well, you know. They wanted to tell you they cared. Why did you run off?"

"I just . . . I was . . ." Grandpa reached across the table and took my hand. It helped me finish what I was saying. "I was afraid I'd cry again. I didn't want them to see me cry."

Grandma rubbed her forehead harder and bit her lip. Grandpa squeezed my hand tighter. We were all three trying not to cry again.

After supper we sat in the living room, each one of us with a book. I read the same page of *Calico Captive* three times before I realized it, and I didn't think either Grandma or Grandpa had turned a single page. The television might help. At least it would add some sound to the house besides the ticking clock that was louder than I ever remembered it. But somehow turning on *The Ed Sullivan Show* didn't seem right tonight.

Around eight-thirty I decided to go to bed. Once I got there it took forever to fall asleep. All I could think about was Mary Kate, and that got me tossing and turning in that squeaky bed until the sheets were bunched up at my feet. I wished I were in my own big bed back home, where Mama and Daddy's room was right across the hall. *There I go wishing again, and that isn't good.*

I switched the lamp on next to my bed and picked up the journal Daddy had given me before he left. It was one of those composition notebooks with the marbly black-and-white covers that teachers tell you to write essays in. "This is for writing down your adventures during the summer," Daddy said. "I'll write you and Mama letters about what I'm doing in Germany, and when I get home, you can show me what you've written."

How could I possibly write down what we had been doing today? Daddy should have been here with us through every minute. I knew he had to do what the air force said, but it just wasn't right that he was so far away when we needed him.

I turned the light off, closed my eyes tight, and decided to try counting sheep. How do people count sheep, anyway? Do they picture them standing in line and going through a little gate one at a time? At the Millers' sheep pen, there were so many packed in that they looked like dirty puffs of wool all matted together. They didn't smell too good, either. Maybe baby lambs would be cleaner little puffs of wool and easier to count, but they wouldn't stay still for long or move very far from their mothers. And I was right back to thinking of Mary Kate so far away from Mama.

Through the open window I listened to the distant gurgling of the creek. Every now and then, louder than the sound of the water, was the high trill of a screech owl, almost like a baby's cry. Was it coming from the graveyard? I thought of Mama in her hospital room all by herself and about my rock baby resting in the V of the tree beside the creek.

The next thing I knew, it was morning, and Grandma was already up in her big, sunny kitchen. Her white hair looked like she had just been to the beauty parlor, and she wore a Sunday dress with her green checked apron tied around it.

"Why are you dressed up, Grandma?" I asked.

"We're bringing your mama home today. I thought it

would make her feel better if we spruced up for her."
Grandma had cooked fried eggs the way I liked them
with the yolks broken and hard, not soupy. She spooned
buttery grits on the plate and poured me a big glass of
orange juice, twice as much as I usually got. It tasted
good.

"After you eat, you can help me pack away all the
baby clothes and blankets."

"Why?" I asked.

Grandma sighed so loudly I could hear it all the way
across the kitchen. "We're donating them to the hospital
nursery," she said. "There's a local family that already has
nine children, and the mother just had twins. I'm sure the
family could use new baby clothes."

I pictured the tiny gowns and soft blankets that Mama
had been working on for months. "All of them? Couldn't
I keep some?"

"Well, Annie, whatever would you do with baby
clothes? You gave up dolls years ago, and you never
much liked them. Besides, the clothes would only serve as
another sad reminder to your mama. I'd like them gone
before she gets home."

"But what if she has another baby?" I asked.

Grandma just looked at me for a moment before answering. "She couldn't go through this again. We *all*
couldn't go through this again. Annie, please don't ask
me any more questions right now. It's too hard."

"Sorry," I muttered. Yes, it *was* hard for everyone,

including me, and I didn't see how giving away all those beautiful clothes would make it better.

There had been at least two other babies who had never even gotten as far along as Mary Kate. I was younger then, so no one really explained it to me. I guess they thought kids didn't listen to whispers, but the second time was only two years ago, and I heard Mama and Daddy talking about a miscarriage. Mama had walked around the house with a tissue wadded in her hand. Her eyes were red and swollen for days, even weeks.

This time was different. In the spring, Mama announced, "We're having a baby." And when Mama was happy, it was impossible for anyone around her not to be excited, too.

Right from the start people asked me, "Do you want a brother or a sister?" I'd always say it didn't matter because that was what Mama and Daddy said. Now I couldn't figure out why I had secretly wished for a sister. I'd have loved a little brother just as much.

Grandma sat down at the table with a cup of coffee while I finished my eggs. My thoughts shifted back to the baby clothes, and I decided to risk asking one more question. "What about the blanket I made? Couldn't I save that?"

It was a pale yellow flannel with daisies embroidered in each corner. Mama had taught me to blanket-stitch, and I'd worked my way around the entire edge. My lines looked more like crooked teeth than Mama's neat little fence-row stitches, but I spent an hour each day for a full week and even embroidered my initials in one corner. Mama said I did a better job than she herself had when she had first learned to sew.

"I suppose you could keep that one," Grandma said, after she swallowed the last of her coffee. "You can save it for your hope chest."

Hope chest. I didn't feel very hopeful. But, yes, maybe this blanket could be the first thing to put in my hope chest—if I ever got one. I was not *wishing* anymore, but maybe I could hope.

"Clear your plate," Grandma said with another big sigh. "It's time we packed the baby clothes."

When Grandma had everything spread out on the bed, it reminded me of the fat pattern envelope Mama had bought at the fabric store—the one with the pictures of everything you could make for a newborn baby. The pattern was called "A Complete Baby Layette" and included bonnets with ruffled brims, gowns with drawstring bottoms so the baby's feet wouldn't get cold, short and long jackets that tied with little bows down the front, and warm, snuggly buntings for the winter. Our baby wouldn't need a bunting in Florida, so that was the only thing Mama didn't make.

She had pulled everything out and spread the pieces of thin paper across the dining room table. Then she started pinning and cutting. Soon little bits of thread and piles of pastel fabric scraps lay everywhere, mostly greens and yellows so it could be for either a boy or a girl. It wasn't fair that girls weren't supposed to get blue, but I could understand that boys would think pink was a sissy color. Mama did make one sky-blue jacket, though, and drew a colt on the front, just like a picture from my old book *The Little Fellow*. Then we both took turns embroidering it in the outline stitch. It was my favorite of all the jackets.

One by one, Grandma and I folded the clothes and blankets and packed them into two big white cardboard boxes. They were washed and ironed, all ready for a new baby. I couldn't resist pressing my face into the little blue jacket on top and breathing in the fresh scent of Ivory Snow.

"Here's the yellow blanket. You did a good job on it, Annie," Grandma said. She looked like she might start to cry when she tucked in the last gown, smoothed it over with her hand, and shut the lid.

The closed box made me think about the little pile of red clay in the church graveyard. I hugged myself to keep from shivering.

As soon as Grandma went back to the kitchen, I lifted the box lid, pulled out the tiny blue jacket, and put it in a drawer, along with the yellow blanket. Those little twins in the hospital wouldn't miss one piece of clothing. They were pretty lucky to be getting everything else. After all, the clothes were supposed to be for Mary Kate.

About an hour later, Grandma and I walked down the

same hospital hallway as we had yesterday, but this time my sneakers didn't tap on the floor the way my white loafers had. I thought about those ruined loafers, washed somewhere down the creek. Would some other girl find them along the bank? Or would they float into a river and then another bigger river until they finally reached the ocean? I was carrying one of the boxes of baby clothes and trying to think of anything but seeing Mama again. Maybe I should have waited in the car with Grandpa. I missed Mama, but at the same time, I didn't know what to say to her when she was still so sad.

We stopped at the nurses' desk to give them the clothes. The two nurses smiled and said thank you over and over. "This is so generous of you."

Grandma walked away before they finished talking. I went over to the window of the nursery and saw the little twins, snuggled into bassinets side by side. One was wrapped in a pink blanket and the other was wrapped in blue. An empty bassinet stood in the corner. Had that been Mary Kate's?

The nurses whispered behind me. "Life doesn't make sense," one said. "Two healthy babies, the second a surprise for a family that can barely feed the nine mouths they already have."

"And that other woman in yonder with her milk coming in for all it's worth," the second nurse added.

"Poor soul even asked to hold her baby after it died, you know," the first nurse said.

"I heard that." The other nurse sighed. "You'd think

the doctor might ignore hospital regulations for once, wouldn't you?"

"Might have done her some good. Too bad she can't help feed one of those twins."

Hospital regulations. I hated even the sound of the words. Whoever made them up had no feelings. I was sure Mama needed to hold Mary Kate for the same reason I needed to hold my rock baby: to take away that awful empty feeling inside. Maybe Mama *could* hold one of the twins. In fact . . .

They must have noticed me because there was a quick "shushing" sound, and when I turned around, the nurses pretended they were busy reading papers spread out on the big desk. I knew I wasn't supposed to hear their conversation, but what they had said gave me an idea. Why should one family get two babies when they didn't even need one? I felt a flicker of hope.

I slipped down the hall to Mama's room. Inside, Grandma was helping her into the flowered maternity dress she had worn two days before. Even zipped, the dress hung loose in front. Mama looked up and half smiled when I came in, but the smile faded away real quick.

Grabbing her hand, I said, "Mama, maybe that other family would give us one of their babies—even the little boy. The nurse said they had too many mouths to feed. We could adopt–"

"Annie!" Grandma almost yelled my name. "That's

nonsense. No family would give up their baby. Hush up now."

"But—"

"No, Annie," Grandma said in her most determined voice.

It was like a slap in the face. My cheeks burned and my eyes stung with tears. All I could do was ball my hands into fists. For a second I had seen a little spark in Mama's eyes, like a bright light that flickered out. Then it was like a shade came down over them.

"It's okay, dear," Mama said in a soft voice. "I know you meant well, but that family loves their babies. They'll figure out a way to take care of them." She put her hand out, but didn't quite touch my cheek.

I squeezed my hands even tighter so my fingernails dug into my skin.

A different nurse, big and all businesslike, pushed an empty wheelchair into the room. "Good morning, Mrs. Winters," she said. "I know you must want to get home. It's a bright day outside, just like a shiny penny."

Who cares about a shiny day? Doesn't the nurse know anything?

Mama nodded and sat down in the wheelchair. Grandma picked up Mama's overnight suitcase with her left hand and took my hand in her right, like I was a five-year-old who didn't know any better. We followed the nurse and the wheelchair out.

No one said anything, not even when we got down to

the front entrance of the hospital, where Grandpa waited in the station wagon. The silence roared in my ears, louder than a whole crowd of people talking. Grandpa got out, opened the front door for Mama, and tucked her in. Grandma sat in the backseat next to me.

I looked down at the dents my fingernails had made in the palms of my hands. I could still feel them hurting. The whole way home I looked out the window, thinking about those two babies in the nursery—Mama holding one and me holding the other one.

Chapter Three

Back at the house, while Grandma settled Mama into the rocking chair in front of the empty fireplace, I sneaked into the bedroom. Grabbing the yellow baby blanket from the dresser drawer, I stuffed it under my shirt so Grandma wouldn't ask what I was doing with it, and took off down the driveway. At the bottom, I crossed the road and continued down the steep path to the creek, anxious to hold my rock baby wrapped safely in the soft flannel. The emptiness inside me was growing again.

At first I couldn't find the V of the twin tree where I

had left my rock baby, and my heart started to pound. There were too many rhododendron bushes with their wilting white blossoms, and no double tree. *Oh, wait a minute. I was much farther upstream.* I took a deep breath and slowed down.

Following the creek bank, I scrambled across slippery rocks, dodged trees, and stepped over rotten logs. The ground was slick and covered with moss in places I was sure the sun never got to. My shoes were muddy again, but it didn't matter this time since I was wearing old sneakers and blue jeans. Even if I slid down the boulders on my bottom and rubbed a hole in my pants, no one would mind.

Finally I reached the big flat rock and saw the twin tree with the rhododendron bush behind it. My rock baby was there–right in the V where I'd left it. *Oh, thank goodness for that.* I touched it before I pulled the blanket from under my shirt and spread it out on the rock. Then I picked up the rock baby with my hand supporting the back, just like I would have held Mary Kate or one of those twin babies, and placed it on the blanket. I wrapped it like a hot dog in a bun and picked it up again.

Holding it this way with just a little bit of the rock peeking out of the top of the blanket made it easier to pretend the rock baby was real. I kissed it lightly and then held it against my shoulder. It felt just right. Part of a lullaby kept running through my mind. I couldn't remember the words Mama used to sing to me, but I did remember the tune, and I hummed along with the sound of the creek.

I don't know how long I stood there rocking and humming, but at some point I became aware of two noisy cardinals—one a bright red male and the other a brownish female with a red beak, flying around and chattering back and forth. They squawked louder and louder.

When I looked to see what was bothering them, there was the same woman I had seen yesterday. She wasn't close enough for me to see her clearly, but I could tell she was wearing the floppy sunbonnet that hid her face even in the shade. The woman carried a basket this time and bent down to the ground every now and then. What was she doing? She couldn't be picking blackberries, it was too early. Besides, berries grew out in sunny spots. The woman moved steadily up the hill, stopping once or twice to pick something up, and finally disappeared.

This time I was going to investigate, but I had to take care of my rock baby first. I unwrapped it, gave it a quick kiss, and placed it back in its V cradle with a little pat. There was no clean, dry place to leave my yellow blanket, so I folded it and stuffed it back under my shirt. Then I was off to investigate the mysterious woman.

The bank was steeper here, and I had to be careful not to slide down into the creek. The rush of the water was growing louder, and the air was cooler. I knew this meant I was closer to the big waterfall. Scrambling over a few more boulders, I finally came to the outline of the woman's shoeprints in the mud. My own shoes fit into them with room to spare.

Dodging a bee buzzing around my head, I followed the footprints away from the creek and back and forth to little clumps of mushrooms. That must be what the woman was gathering.

The footprints led to a wider trail. And looking way to the top of the path, up near the road, I spotted a house. Not a big one—in fact, more like an unpainted shack. The closer I got, the more familiar it looked. *Then I realized it was the little house across from the road to Tater Hill.*

I had never approached it from the back before, so maybe that was why I didn't recognize it at first. The tiny house sat just off the edge of Loggers Creek Road. When cars drove by, dust sprayed across its crooked porch and over the broken rocking chair, coating it all with a haze of dirty red. For as long as I could remember that house had been empty, the windows boarded up. Grandpa called it the McGee house. As each summer passed and I grew older, the house seemed to grow smaller and lonelier.

"Why doesn't someone live in that poor house?" I remembered asking Grandma when I was about eight.

"Something bad happened there years and years ago," she said. "But it was long before your grandpa and I moved here to North Carolina."

"What do you mean *bad*?" I asked. The investigator in me kept asking questions.

"I won't add gossip to something I know nothing about," Grandma answered with that look on her face that meant it wasn't a subject for children. "But don't you go near that place on your own."

Bobby would know, I remember thinking. And, sure enough, he told me, "A murderer used to live there, at least thirty years ago, and now *she's* in prison."

From then on I always thought of it as the murderer's house. And now that I knew which house this was, I was feeling more and more nervous and out of breath from climbing the steep hill. Should I keep going? I stopped to think, crouching low to the ground. The footprints led to the back door, and the door was open, but there was no sound of anyone moving around inside. I told myself the woman couldn't be the murderer. *She* was in prison . . . or maybe even dead by now. Thirty years was a long time. Was the woman even real? Maybe she was a ghost. I hadn't really gotten a good look at her. The footprints were real, that was for sure. My own shoe had fit right into them.

Well, I wasn't brave enough to look inside, so I sneaked around the outside, hoping I could catch a glimpse of her through a window. But the windows were still boarded up. And there was a stink—old and rotten, the way mushrooms smelled deep in the woods where there's no sun. It wasn't the kind of place I wanted to stay around for long.

Then the noise started. A banging sound. Not like a

hammer, but like wood hitting wood, over and over and over . . .

I froze.

Once I caught my breath, I couldn't get away from there fast enough. At least I was racing downhill instead of uphill this time. It didn't take too long, but my heart was pounding, both from the running and the fear, when I slipped around the back of Grandma and Grandpa's house and across the yard to my swing that hung from the big branch on the hickory tree.

If only there were someone I could talk to about the mysterious woman—but I didn't dare tell Mama or Grandma. First of all, they had too much on their minds, and second, I wasn't even supposed to go near there. Even Grandpa might get mad at me for going near that house.

The rhythm of the banging wood still beat in my head as I swayed back and forth on the swing. When I looked down, I remembered my yellow baby blanket. The front of my shirt lay flat against my stomach. The baby blanket was gone.

"I can't lose that blanket!" I said out loud. Not all those tiny stitches I spent so many hours on. But more than that, it was the only thing I had made for Mary Kate all by myself. And now I needed it for my rock baby. I tried to remember it falling out while I was running, but I had no memory of that—only of trying to get away from the banging sound as fast as I could. Maybe I'd find it lying somewhere along the road before I got too close to the murderer's house. It would be dirty, probably coated in red dust, but I could wash it.

Heading back across the yard and around the side of the house, I ran straight into Grandpa.

"There you are, Annie," he said. "What have you been up to?"

"Grandpa." I looked at him, ready to blurt out the whole story of the yellow blanket and the mysterious woman and the murderer's house. But I couldn't. Grandpa was bent over and tired, like much more than two days had passed since Mary Kate died. I couldn't make him worry about me being where I shouldn't be.

"Yes?" Grandpa waited.

"Nothing," I muttered, focusing on the ground. "I mean, I . . ."

"Grandma has lunch just about ready," Grandpa said before I could think of anything else to say. "Go in and wash up. And better take your shoes off outside."

"Okay." I untied my muddy sneakers, slipped them off, and left them next to Grandpa's work boots. The blanket would have to wait until after lunch. I hoped no one else would find it.

While I was washing up, the telephone rang in the hallway. I could hear Grandma answer it.

"Oh, Robert. I've been trying to get hold of you. . . ."

Daddy. In a flash I was standing next to Grandma.

"Can I talk to him?" I said. "Please . . . just for a minute?"

Grandma shook her head and motioned me away.

"But I need to talk to him." I was sure just hearing his voice would make me feel better.

Grandma covered the telephone receiver with her hand and said, "Go get your mama right now, Annie. She's in the living room. Your daddy's calling all the way from Germany."

"But—"

"Right now," Grandma repeated. "You know how expensive a long-distance call is."

There was no use arguing with Grandma. I went to the living room and was surprised Mama hadn't heard the phone ring. She was sitting in the rocking chair, holding an ice pack to her chest and staring into the empty fireplace.

"It's Daddy," I said, and Mama jumped as if I had sneaked up behind her.

When Mama reached the phone, Grandma pulled me away with her to the kitchen. I couldn't even stand there next to Mama and try to hear Daddy's voice through the receiver.

"They need their privacy," Grandma said.

"But I want to talk to him, too."

"I know, but not this time. Not when it's long-distance from Germany."

"Then when can I ever talk to him?"

"You can write him a letter, dear, and I'm sure he'll write back."

I sat at my place at the table and stirred my tomato soup, just to have something to do with my hands. Writing wouldn't be the same. I had only written one thing in my journal right after we got here to North Carolina, and I hadn't been able to write down anything since then, so how could I write a letter? If only I could *talk* to Daddy, I knew he would come back and take us home to Florida where we could be together again. Things would be almost normal, even though we wouldn't have Mary Kate.

Grandpa sat down at the table, too, but none of us ate. The grilled cheese sandwiches grew cold on our plates while we waited.

"That telephone call will cost a fortune," Grandma said.

Money. Didn't Grandma know that some things are more important than money?

When Mama finally came to the table, her eyes were red and swollen again, the only color in her white face. She didn't say anything until Grandma asked what I was dying to know.

"Is Robert coming home?"

Mama shook her head. "He said he would come if I needed him. The air force would fly him back here, but I told him not to." She covered her eyes with her hand and mumbled, "There's nothing he can do now anyway."

"But I want him to come," I blurted out. "I need him."

Mama looked surprised to hear my voice. "Annie, it's too far, and he'd just have to go right back again. I couldn't stand it if he came home only to . . ." Mama didn't finish the sentence. Her chin was trembling.

I didn't want to see her cry again. Grown-ups weren't supposed to cry. I jumped out of my chair and headed for the door. Before it closed, I heard Grandpa say, "Let her go."

Outside I shoved my feet into my sneakers, tied them as fast as I could, and began to retrace my steps.

My yellow blanket and my rock baby. Those were the two things I needed. Then maybe I could think about Daddy and how far away he was. And how Mama wasn't Mama anymore.

The blanket wasn't in the driveway, and it wasn't lying in the road. Heading steadily uphill, I searched through the daisies and tiger lilies and touch-me-nots that grew wild along the side of Loggers Creek Road. A car passed, blowing a cloud of dust around my face. I held my nose and closed my eyes until the car was gone and the dirt had settled. Then I went on looking. I couldn't let myself think of anything but finding the blanket.

The murderer's house was in sight when I finally rounded the third hairpin curve. Crossing to the far side of the road, I pretended I was just walking past while I looked for the blanket. Then I turned around and walked back. No sign of the blanket anywhere, and the front of the house was still boarded up, just like the side was. It looked empty. And I didn't hear the sound of banging wood. Maybe the mysterious woman had left.

At any rate, I still needed to find the blanket. Taking a deep breath to store up all my courage, I crept back along the side of the house with my eyes on the ground instead of straight ahead.

A soft, raspy voice asked, "Is this what you're looking for?"

Chapter Four

Her shoes were the first thing I saw—men's shoes, scuffed, laced up, and too big for the skinny legs that stuck out beneath a long skirt, so faded it had no color. I didn't know what kind of face I expected, but maybe more like a witch's. Definitely not like the one I saw looking back at me. The woman's skin was as delicate as tissue paper crisscrossed with fine lines, like creases that had been folded in and then smoothed out. Her hair was brown, streaked with gray, and drawn back from her face in a long braid that hung over her shoulder. She looked tired and her skin was pale, as if she hadn't seen the sun any more than those mushrooms she collected.

There, dangling from the fingers of her right hand, was my yellow baby blanket. The woman asked again, "Is this what you're looking for, child?" Her clear gray eyes peered at me like a kitten's, timid, but mostly curious.

I knew I should grab the blanket and run, but something about this woman kept me there. I nodded before I managed to say, "Yes, ma'am." My mouth felt like I had swallowed a cotton ball.

Before I could grasp the blanket, the woman took the other edge with her left hand and spread it out to its full width. "A right nice piece with all that fine handiwork. Did you stitch it yourself?" she asked.

"Yes, ma'am." I licked my lips and reached out again for the blanket.

Now the woman bunched up one corner and ran her fingers over the initials I had embroidered. "A.E.W.," she read aloud. "What do they stand for?"

My voice squeaked when I answered. "Annabel Elizabeth Winters." Was I going to get my blanket back? Was I strong enough to pull it away from the woman and run with it, if I had to? I didn't think she was the murderer, but who could she be?

"Ah, Annabel. A beautiful name." The woman closed her eyes and tilted her head back, as if she was remembering something.

No one had ever called my name beautiful before. It

always made me think of stiff old ladies, since everyone said it was an old-fashioned name. I didn't know any other Annabel, except for the great-grandmother I was named after but who had died before I was born.

The woman started talking again, but I wasn't sure she was speaking to me. With her eyes still closed, she spoke more like she was reciting a poem than just talking. "It was many and many a year ago, in a kingdom by the sea. That a maiden there lived whom you may know by the name of Annabel Lee."

I was sure I could grab the blanket now if I wanted to, even if the woman opened her eyes. I was almost as tall and pretty sure I was almost as strong. But as soon as the woman said the name Annabel, I wanted to hear more of the poem. The woman continued in a rhythm and a voice that sounded like music . . .

> *"And this maiden she lived with no other thought*
> *Than to love and be loved by me.*
>
> *She was a child and I was a child,*
> *In this kingdom by the sea,*
> *But we loved with a love that was more than love—*
> *I and my Annabel Lee—*
> *With a love that the wingéd seraphs of Heaven*
> *Coveted her and me."*

"Wingéd seraphs" sounded like some sort of birds or maybe angels, something to do with heaven. I pictured them peeking down over the edge of a cloud at the beautiful Annabel standing on the seashore. Now the woman opened her eyes and stopped speaking, as if she were surprised to see me standing there instead of the other Annabel.

I waited for a few moments, silently asking to hear more of the story. The woman seemed to know what I was thinking, because she carefully folded the blanket and held it up against her as she continued . . .

> *"And this was the reason that, long ago,*
> *In this kingdom by the sea,*
> *A wind blew out of a cloud by night*
> *Chilling my Annabel Lee;*
> *So that her highborn kinsmen came*
> *And bore her away from me,*
> *To shut her up in a sepulchre*
> *In this kingdom by the sea."*

The words made me shiver, and I thought about the small mound of red clay just inside the church graveyard. Mary Kate would be as alone there as Annabel Lee was in her grave by the sea. I missed part of the poem, thinking about my baby sister, but I started listening again in time to hear:

> *"But our love it was stronger by far than the love*
> *Of those who were older than we—*
> *Of many far wiser than we—*

And neither the angels in Heaven above
Nor the demons down under the sea,
Can ever dissever my soul from the soul
Of the beautiful Annabel Lee.

For the moon never beams without bringing me dreams
Of the beautiful Annabel Lee;
And the stars never rise but I see the bright eyes
Of the beautiful Annabel Lee;
And so, all the night-tide, I lie down by the side
Of my darling, my darling, my life and my bride,
In her sepulchre there by the sea—
In her tomb by the side of the sea."

The woman's voice seemed to float around us even after she finished the poem, just like those angels had floated on the clouds above. It *was* a beautiful story and now my name sounded beautiful to me, too.

"Here, child." The woman spread the blanket wide again, leaned forward, and wrapped it around my shoulders as if it were a shawl. "To keep you from taking a chill like the other Annabel." Her hands were rough and red, with blisters on two of her fingers.

"Thank you," I said when she turned to go back into the house. I didn't want her to go, but I didn't know what else to say to her. The woman didn't look or sound like a murderer, and I wanted to know more about the poem.

"Wait," I said, and the woman looked back. "I mean, thank you for the blanket. I thought I lost it."

"It warn't nothing, child. You're not beholden." She turned again to leave.

"That poem," I said. "Did you make it up?"

The woman laughed and shook her head. "No, child. They're the words of Edgar Allan Poe, a hundred or more years ago. Words that took hold of me when I read them, and I set them to memory."

"That's a long poem to remember."

"Not when you've all the time in the world and naught else good to do with it."

"Do you live here?" I asked, wanting to keep the woman talking, more to hear her soft mountain voice and her peculiar way of speaking than anything else.

The woman's eyes looked like a timid kitten's again, and she clasped her rough hands together. "You best be getting on home, child. I'm not much for visiting, and I don't fancy the neighbors knowing I'm here." Then she turned away and disappeared into the dark house.

I stood there with the blanket wrapped around my shoulders, thinking of the beautiful Annabel and the musical words of the poem. I wondered how long the woman had lived in this tiny house with no sunlight shining through the boarded-up windows and that rotten mushroom smell seeping out of it.

After a few minutes, the banging sound started up again. It didn't scare me this time. Maybe the woman was building something or, more likely, fixing something. The whole house looked like it needed fixing. The banging sound had a regular beat to it—a bang swoosh bang, bang swoosh bang—like the rhythm and the rhyming of the Annabel poem.

I wished I could remember all the words instead of just bits and pieces. There was something about the moonbeams bringing him dreams of the beautiful Annabel Lee. And the stars in the sky like the bright eyes of the beautiful Annabel Lee. What was the poet's name? Edgar Allan Poe? Maybe Grandpa had a book of his poems somewhere in his bookshelves. I decided I'd look for it when I got home.

But first I followed the path down to the creek so I could hold my rock baby while I thought about the mysterious woman with all the time in the world and naught else good to do with it.

Chapter Five

Rain started that night and continued for three days straight. The soft sound rattling on the roof soothed me to sleep. But during the day it dampened down more than the leaves on the trees and the grass on the ground. A cloud had settled over the mountain, cloaking the house in fog. When I looked out the window, all I could see were the hemlock trees closest to the house and the blue station wagon, barely distinguishable in the driveway. Beyond that was nothingness. I felt as if the four of us in the house were the only people in the world, wrapped in a sadness as thick as the fog.

What was Bobby doing through all this rain? Had the Millers gotten the hay cut and into the barn before the rain started? For sure their house would be crowded and noisy on a day like this. That would be good. If only I could slip in unnoticed, I would put on my raincoat and walk down there, just to feel a part of a big family. But if Caroline and Ruthie were around, they'd be asking more questions, and I didn't want that.

Instead, I searched the tall living room bookcase for a poetry book. I couldn't reach the top shelves without getting a chair from the kitchen, but I read the titles of every book on the bottom four shelves. Mostly they were old textbooks for math and chemistry and physics. Grandpa had been a high school math and science teacher before he retired, and he must have saved every textbook he ever used. I did find the volume of Shakespeare's plays that Mama had read aloud from last summer before we went to see *The Merchant of Venice* at the college. But no Edgar Allan Poe.

The entire time I searched, Mama sat in the rocking chair in front of the cold fireplace and didn't seem to notice I was in the room. Her hair, which used to be a shiny golden brown, hung stringy and limp around her face. She seemed to be growing smaller, curling into herself, and she wore her maternity clothes because that was all she'd brought with her from home. Grandma's wool sweater hung over her shoulders, and she still held an ice pack to her chest. Every now and then, Mama patted the ice pack just like she was burping a baby. I wondered if the ice pack was as good to hold as my rock baby was, and that made me wish my rock baby was hidden in my room, instead of all the way down by the creek. Then I realized I was *wishing* again and made myself stop.

I yanked the Shakespeare book from its place on the shelf and held it right in front of Mama. "Here's the book with all the plays," I said, trying to get her attention. "We could read *A Midsummer Night's Dream*, Mama. You said that was the play for this summer's Shakespeare Festival. Remember? We'll be going to see it pretty soon, right?"

Mama looked up, but not into my eyes. "Oh, I don't know," she said.

"Do you want me to ask Grandpa to build a fire to keep you warm?"

Mama shook her head.

"How about some music? I could put a record on." I was already over at Grandpa's hi-fi set, looking through his stack of records. "You always tell me that music by Bach or Mozart puts your mind in order."

"No music," Mama said. "Not now, Annie."

No music? Mama always wanted music—either playing the piano herself or listening to a record on the hi-fi—classical, of course, not rock 'n' roll. Sometimes I got tired of it, but she never did. Now I wished we had a whole orchestra playing right here in the living room. That would make her sit up and take notice.

I plunked the heavy Shakespeare book on the floor

next to the rocking chair. Maybe after a while, Mama would pick it up and start reading. Then I headed downstairs to Grandpa's basement workshop. Grandpa would talk to me no matter what he was doing.

It was bright inside the workshop even though there were no windows. A long fluorescent light beamed down over the workbench, and a small fire crackled in the pot-bellied stove, lifting the dampness from the room. Thin curls of reddish wood littered the floor, like strawberry blond ringlets of hair that had been cut at a barbershop. I breathed in the fresh, woody smell.

Grandpa stood at his bench, running his plane along the edge of a board, making more wooden ringlets that scattered to the floor. He didn't hear me and kept working, his eyes fixed on the wood. Little bits of sawdust rested on his glasses and across his nose. He hadn't shaved for three days now, and his chin was scruffier than ever.

"What are you making, Grandpa?"

He turned around with a little jump and then seemed relieved. "Oh, Annie, good, it's you," he said.

"You've started something new." I touched the smooth wood. "What is it?"

I loved to watch Grandpa build a piece of furniture, starting from nothing but flat boards. It was as amazing as watching Mama sew a dress from nothing but a piece of cloth. They both used patterns, cutting and measuring and somehow knowing exactly what they were supposed to do.

"It was meant to be a cradle," Grandpa answered.

"But now I'm not sure what to do with it." He ran his fingers over the same curve of wood I had just touched. "It's my finest cut of cherry. I like cherry best for furniture, that or walnut."

I bent to scoop up a handful of the wood shavings. They were as light as they looked. Curling one around my finger, I said, "You could still make the cradle and save it. Maybe . . ." I didn't quite know what else I wanted to say, but I did know that I didn't want to lose this little curl of wood shaving. It was so fragile, and it gripped my finger just the way Mary Kate would have. I tucked the curl into my pocket.

"Yes, maybe," Grandpa said. "And what have you been up to this rainy morning?"

"I was looking for a book of poems."

"What kind?"

"Oh, poems," I repeated. "Like maybe one by Edgar Allan Poe?"

" 'Quoth the raven, nevermore,' " Grandpa said in surprise.

"One about an Annabel. A beautiful Annabel Lee."

"Oh, that one," Grandpa said. "Let's go upstairs and look."

Grandpa never asked too many questions. But he always listened. "Grandpa," I added. "Would you call me Annabel from now on?"

"Well, Annabel," he said. "I'll try to remember, but please forgive me if I forget. I've had nearly eleven years of Annie."

"I know." I smiled, and it felt good.

Grandpa was tall enough to look through the books on the upper shelves. He pulled out a thick green volume. "Hmmm," he said. "This should have it. It must have been someone's textbook." He skimmed through the table of contents and ran his finger down the lines of page numbers. "Here you go, Annie Annabel. Page seven hundred and sixty-four."

"Thanks, Grandpa." I grabbed the book and vanished to the small bedroom that was mine. The book was called *The American Tradition in Literature,* and on the inside cover was Mama's name before she was married, written in her beautiful penmanship. Marguerite Greenman. I ran my finger over the signature before turning to page 764.

There were lots of things listed by Edgar Allan Poe, twenty-six in all, but that included some short stories, too. I read "Annabel Lee" three times, once out loud, trying to say it the same way the mysterious woman had. My favorite lines were:

> *And neither the angels in Heaven above*
> *Nor the demons down under the sea,*
> *Can ever dissever my soul from the soul*
> *Of the beautiful Annabel Lee.*

It wouldn't be too hard to memorize this poem after all. I read the last few lines over and over until I could say them by heart.

And so, all the night-tide, I lie down by the side
Of my darling, my darling, my life and my bride,
In her sepulchre there by the sea—
In her tomb by the side of the sea.

I was back to thinking about Mary Kate again and her tiny grave beyond the gate. I decided that since Mary Kate didn't have a sepulchre or a tomb, she at least must have a gravestone with her name on it.

That night when I was getting ready for bed, I came across the wood curl in my pants pocket. I wanted to keep it somewhere it wouldn't get swept off the table and lost on the floor. For safekeeping, I opened my journal and pressed it between the pages.

At lunch on the fourth rainy day, which was Friday, Grandma said, "I'm getting cabin fever in the middle of summer. It's time we all got out of this house. Who wants to go for a ride in the car?"

"I do," I said, and then added in a smaller voice, "We could buy a gravestone for Mary Kate."

Both Grandma and Grandpa looked at me in surprise. "Why, Annie, that's a good idea," Grandma said. "We'll have to drive to Hickory for that." She looked at Grandpa. "Do you think it will be as foggy in the valley as it is up here?"

Grandpa shook his head. "They're probably getting rain, but the fog lingers over the mountaintops."

"What do you think, Maggie?" Grandma asked.

Mama was running her fork around her plate. She had barely touched any of her macaroni and cheese. "Hmmm?" She looked up. "What did you say?"

"Annie thought maybe we should go to Hickory to order the gravestone," Grandma said in a careful voice. She opened her eyes wide while she waited for an answer.

Mama seemed to be thinking it over. "Yes, I suppose we should."

"Good," Grandma said, back to her usual brisk voice. "Annie, help me clear the table, please. But we'll leave the dishes till later. It'll take an hour to drive down there."

Grandpa was right about the fog lingering over the mountaintops. When we first started out, it was as if we were moving through a soggy dreamworld with mysterious shapes towering over us. Grandpa drove slower than usual.

Going downhill, our car would suddenly be in the clear, and then, rounding a curve and climbing up, we'd be back in the dense fog. Finally we reached the valley, and the surrounding mountaintops disappeared into nothingness. By the time we arrived in Hickory, the rain had stopped and the sun was trying to break through the high gray clouds.

The sign for the gravestone dealer said, HENDERSON'S STONE CARVING FOR LOVE, FOR REMEMBRANCE, AND FOREVER. Underneath, written in smaller letters, was DESIGNING AND ENGRAVING ON PREMISES.

Mama was slow to get out of the car. Grandma and Grandpa stood on either side of her, Grandpa with his hand on her elbow. Walking ahead, I wandered up and down the rows displaying sample grave markers.

It was set up almost like a miniature graveyard, some stones large, some small, some simple, others intricately carved. A vine-covered arbor marked the entrance to the children's section. Here there were small heart-shaped stones in pinkish granite. Most had lambs or angels hovering over poems.

My favorite was the one with a lamb leaping over the name and BELOVED CHILD written beneath. But Mama chose a plain gray stone with a rounded top. No heart. No animals. No extra words. Only MARY KATE WINTERS with JULY 13–14, 1963 to be carved beneath.

The gravestone would be ready in four weeks. I counted them out in my head. It would be after my birthday and about the time Daddy would come back from Germany and we'd finally go home to Florida. Maybe things would seem normal again by then.

Chapter Six

The drive back up the mountains was like being in another world. The wind had blown away the last wisps of fog. Green meadows, dotted with black cows, stretched steeply up the base of the mountains to the uneven fringe of forests. And the dark woodlands reached upward to touch the blue sky.

Far in the distance I spotted Tater Hill, the one bare mountain with a rounded top, like a peeled potato. Grandma and Grandpa's house was actually partway up a mountain called Doe Ridge, right next to Tater Hill, but that mountain was tree-covered. I could never pick it out in a view from the valley.

As we rode along, my favorite lines from the poem ran over and over through my head, slightly changed. "Can never dissever my soul from the soul / Of the beautiful Annabel Lee." Somehow those words brought me closer to the baby sister I never even got to see. I decided to visit Mary Kate's tiny grave.

When we reached home, Mama went straight to the living room and slumped back into her rocking chair. Grandma tied an apron around her waist and started washing up the lunch dishes. Grandpa headed downstairs to his workshop.

"I'm going back outside," I called to no one in particular.

In the garage, I grabbed an empty canning jar from a shelf and filled it half full from the hose. I wanted to take a bouquet of flowers to Mary Kate's grave, and Sweet Williams were my favorite. They grew at the base of the driveway in clusters of white, pink, and dark-red blossoms that looked like they were already tied into tiny bundles. I was careful to break them off at the base of the stems and arranged them in the jar. Then I continued down the road to the church graveyard.

Mary Kate's little pile of dirt was the first thing I saw just beyond the broken gate. But for some reason, I couldn't walk right over to it. Instead, I started counting the markers—fifty-seven in all—and was careful to step over the messy clumps of long, wet grass that grew across the graves and around the gravestones. I didn't like the ones that had fake plastic flowers propped in front. Beads of water glistened in the new sunshine like thousands of diamonds, making it almost too bright to read the names carved into the stones.

Finally I took a deep breath and stopped at Mary Kate's grave. At least this time no one was around to hear or see me if I cried. The clay had been soaked by the rain and was stained a dark red. A stem of tiny white flowers rested against the mud. *Who had planted the sprig of baby's breath? Grandma? Old Mrs. Miller?*

Kneeling beside the mound, I placed the jar of Sweet Williams at the head of the grave. I tried to picture my baby sister with her light, reddish hair. Would it have been curly or straight? Did she have dark blue eyes like mine, or would they have been brown like Daddy's? When she grew older, would she have had the same sprinkling of freckles over her nose as I did? Would she have liked reading the same books? *I'll never know any of these answers, but Mary Kate will still be a part of me.*

I knew I should be saying some special words aloud, probably words from the Bible. But the only lines I could remember were from the Annabel poem.

"Nothing will ever dissever my soul from the soul of my sister, Mary Kate," I whispered. Then I said it again louder, more like a promise. "Nothing will ever dissever my soul from the soul of my sister, Mary Kate."

I pressed my handprint into the mud on top of the grave—something that would still be there when the dirt dried out and the flowers wilted. Then I broke off a tiny twig of baby's breath and stuck it in my pocket. I'd press it into my journal, along with the wood curl, as another little reminder of Mary Kate.

When I stood to leave, I didn't want to go back home to the silent house where Mama would be in her rocking chair, staring at nothing. How much longer could Mama go on sitting there?

The rushing sound of the creek drew me across the road and through the open meadow. I could see that the creek had overflowed its banks, flooding the rocks with muddy water and flattening the reedy grasses on both sides. I picked my way uphill and into the thick woods. My pant legs were soon soaked from brushing against wet weeds and low bushes.

The woods smelled like earthworms, salamanders, and soggy layers of old leaves. New clumps of mushrooms had sprung up during the past three days of rain. Spongy pillows of moss gleamed emerald green where sunlight filtered through the trees. It was kind of like a magical fairy kingdom—one that I would have liked to show Mary Kate when she was old enough. But now she'd never lie down on spongy moss or look for salamanders under rocks.

At last I came to the big flat rock, barely recognizable with the water washing over it. Resting safely in the V of the tree was the rock baby, stained a blacker gray from the rain. I lifted it carefully, and at the same time the heaviness of the past three days fell off me. For a minute I held the rock baby against my shoulder, patting it lightly on its back, and then I tucked it into the bend of my arm, like a sleeping baby. The yellow blanket was safely folded away in my dresser drawer. I missed having it here, but I couldn't risk losing it again. I'd just have to remember the softness of the blanket around the hardness of the rock.

Walking away from the rushing creek, I realized I was heading uphill toward the murderer's house and the mysterious woman. Snatches of a melody floated on the air above the sound of the water, growing louder the closer I got to the house. Not a song on the radio or notes from a piano, but more like a tune strummed on a guitar. Every now and then a voice sang along.

I was close enough now to see the woman sitting on the back stoop of her house with the door open behind her like a narrow slit leading to a dark cave. She reminded me of a character in some fairy tale I had read years ago—not a scary person, but someone who had lived through hard times. Her head was bent over an instrument that lay across her knees, and her face was hidden by the floppy folds of her sunbonnet. She bobbed her head to the rhythm of the music that she plucked from the strings.

Not sure enough of myself to walk right up to her, I stopped behind the branches of a mountain laurel while she finished her song. I didn't want to scare her, and maybe she didn't want me around; she had said she wasn't much for visiting. But when she pushed the rim of her sunbonnet back from her face and I could see those gray kitten eyes, they didn't seem startled to see me—more like they expected me.

"Annabel," she said in her soft mountain voice.

I loved the sound of my name.

"What is it that you're holding in your arms, child?"

I looked down, almost surprised to see my rock baby. The feel of it was so natural it seemed a part of me. I walked over to the woman and settled myself on the bottom step at her feet. "It's just a rock," I said, holding it out in front of me with both hands. "I like to hold it." Then I changed the subject. "What's that instrument you're playing?"

"A dulcimer," the woman answered. "It was my daddy's. He called it his hog fiddle."

"A *hog* fiddle." The name made me laugh out loud.

"It's sat unused and has gone flat. I've been trying to tune it." The woman pushed her bonnet off her head so that it fell down behind her neck, still tied in front. Her face looked younger today, more of the wrinkles smoothed out with a touch of pink in her cheeks.

"Can you play it without reading music?" I asked.

The woman chuckled. "That's the only way I can play, Annabel. Through listening to the notes in my head or what other people sing. I never had the learning for written music. Nor did my daddy or my granddaddy."

"I can read notes," I said. "But that doesn't mean I can

make them sound right on the piano. My teacher and Mama both say I need to practice more."

"Practicing is good, but to some folk the making of music comes natural. When someone sings a song, you don't have to read the notes to sing along, do you?"

"No."

"Well, that's learning by ear. Here, you try the hog fiddle."

"Really?" I set my rock baby on the step next to me, reached for the dulcimer, and set it across my knees. It was longer than the full length of my arm, narrow in the middle, and curved wider at both ends like an hourglass. Four heart-shaped holes were cut out of the smooth, dark wood, and three strings stretched along a narrow board, which ran the length of the instrument.

"You can pluck the strings one at a time," she said, reaching her right hand over my shoulder to show me. "This is the melody string, the middle, and the base. Or you can strum a chord." This time she leaned down and pressed on two of the strings with a small stick held in her left hand and flicked her right fingers across all three strings. "You try."

I plucked and strummed on my own, but the sounds I made weren't very musical.

"Slide the stick up and down the frets, those little ridges, to make more of a melody of different chords. Mind you, it does take practice."

"It would take me an awful lot of practice," I said. "Would you play me a song? That might help."

The woman placed the dulcimer back across her lap. "I'm a tad rusty," she said, clearing her throat. She strummed across the strings a few times, trying out some chords, then flowed into a song. The beautiful, haunting sound was amazing. I knew enough from piano lessons that the minor key gave the music its sadness. But the woman's voice was clear as water and bottomless as a well. It reached right into me and filled the empty hole.

"I'm just a poor wayfaring stranger,
A-travelin' through this world of woe.
But there's no sickness, toil, or danger
In that bright world to which I go.
I'm goin' there to see my father.
I'm goin' there no more to roam.
I'm just a-goin' over Jordan.
I'm just a-goin' over home."

Inching up a step to sit next to her, I picked up my rock again and nestled it into my arms. The strange, lonely song seemed to fit this mysterious woman. The words held so much feeling that I was sure she was singing about the sorrow in her own life. I watched her knobby fingers move up and down the fretboard. Would I ever be able to play like that without any notes to follow?

When the sad song was over, the woman said, "How about a happier tune? It'll take but a minute to tighten my melody string." She turned the peg, plucked the string, turned the peg a bit tighter, and plucked again. "Still a tad flat, but it'll do," she said and slid right into "Fly in the buttermilk, shoo fly shoo! Fly in the buttermilk, shoo fly shoo! Fly in the buttermilk, shoo fly shoo! Skip to my Lou, my darling." This was one I knew and joined in singing all the verses while I bounced the rock on my knee and tapped my foot to the rhythm.

We both laughed at the end, and suddenly I realized this was the first time I had been happy since Mary Kate had died. Good thing no one lived close enough to hear us singing and making so much noise.

The woman pressed her hand down on the strings to silence them. "Child, you hold that rock just like it was a baby."

Her words surprised me, and a sudden lump grew in my throat. I fought back tears. No one—not Grandma or Grandpa or Mama—had actually talked about the baby all week. They had talked around the subject—about the gravestone and the baby clothes and things that weren't so important. Mama hadn't talked at all. No one mentioned Mary Kate, or how sad we all were; how all our hopes had died along with her.

"It's my rock baby," I said in a whisper that caught on that lump.

"What did you say, child?"

"My rock baby," I repeated. Once I started, it was easier to go on. "It's because my baby sister was born too soon. She died almost a week ago, before I even got a chance to see her. When I hold my rock, things seem all right again. I can close my eyes and believe I'm really holding her and that nothing can happen to her as long as I'm right here." It was good to actually say it aloud. Tears slipped out along with my words and slid down my face. I tasted their saltiness on my tongue. For some reason, I didn't mind crying in front of this woman.

"Oh, Annabel." She sighed and wrapped her arm around my shoulders. "And that yellow blanket you stitched so fine was for your baby sister, warn't it?"

I nodded, and in that instant I realized how much I missed Mama. Not only her arms around me, but also talking to her and having her listen.

We sat there like that for a few moments in silence, and then the woman took my rock baby in her own arms. "You're right, child. It does feel like a baby." She closed her eyes and spoke in the same voice she had used when she recited the poem. "He shall feed his flock like a shepherd. He shall gather the lambs with his arm, and carry them in his bosom, and gently lead those that are with young."

"Is that another poem?" I asked.

The woman shook her head. "From the Bible," she said. "Those are the words that comforted me when I lost my baby boy. From the Book of Isaiah, chapter forty, verse eleven. Not all the other words the preacher spoke. Only those. I could picture the Lord carrying my baby in his arms close to his heart, just as a shepherd would carry a newborn lamb. He would be safe there, safe from all the woes of this world."

I closed my eyes and tried to picture my little sister being held safe in God's arms. It would have helped if I had seen Mary Kate and knew exactly what she looked like and what God looked like, but it did comfort me to think of a shepherd holding a baby lamb. "Did you hold your baby before he died?" I asked.

The woman nodded. "All through the night."

"Mama wanted to hold Mary Kate, but they wouldn't let her."

"No one has the right to keep a woman from holding her child."

"That's what I thought." It made me feel good that a grown-up agreed with me. "What was his name? Your baby, I mean."

"Isaiah. I called him Isaiah after the Bible verse. It was a good name for him."

"Isaiah McGee?" I asked. "Grandpa always calls this the McGee house."

Now the woman looked surprised by my question. She was silent for a moment and breathed a deep breath before she answered. "Yes, he was Isaiah McGee."

"And are you Mrs. McGee?" I asked.

She hesitated again, as if trying to decide before answering me. "McGee was my name only by marriage. And that's not been for many years. You can call me Miss Eliza, if you'd like, Annabel."

"*Miss Eliza,*" I repeated, happy that I could finally give her a name. "Are you all alone here?"

She nodded. "Aloneness don't trouble me none, child. I'd as soon be alone as have neighbors looking in on me. That I wouldn't fancy."

"But what about me?" I didn't want to think about Miss Eliza being all alone in this dark little house without any friends. And I was sure she could not have been the murderer who used to live here. "I could look in on you," I said. "I could help you fix your house and take the boards off your windows. Don't you want some light in your house?"

Miss Eliza smiled. "Yes, Annabel, I'd be much obliged. I'd like some light in my house."

Chapter Seven

Bobby walked up to visit on Saturday afternoon. Even though it had only been six days since I'd last seen him, he looked different—older somehow. He had slicked back his thick, curly hair with water, or maybe even Brylcreem. I could smell something perfumy, and he seemed nervous standing at the door.

With all that had happened I knew I had changed, too, but I didn't think I looked different on the outside. I wouldn't tell anyone about the rock baby, but I *might* tell Bobby about Miss Eliza—if he promised to keep it secret.

"Do you want to come in?" I asked.

"Sure," Bobby said.

We headed for the living room, and I immediately regretted it. Mama was slumped in her rocking chair—just the way she always was now—not moving, just staring. I could see Bobby's surprise—more like shock.

"Hey, Miz Winters," he mumbled.

Mama moved a little and nodded her head, but didn't answer. Bobby glanced at me for a second before looking down at his feet.

"Let's go back outside," I said, suddenly wanting to get away from Mama, from Bobby, from this whole place. I had never been embarrassed by Mama before.

"Why did you come up?" I asked Bobby once we were out on the porch.

"Just wondered what you've been doing all week."

"Not much," I said. It had never been hard to talk to Bobby before. Maybe I wouldn't tell him about Miss Eliza. "You can see what this house has been like all week, and you know it rained every day. I read some. I thought maybe you'd come up here to play cards one day."

"Mamaw said not to be a bother . . . 'cause of . . . well, you know . . ."

"You can say it out loud, Bobby! It's because the baby died. My little sister, who I never even got to see, died, and everyone is sad, but no one wants to talk about it." I stopped to take a breath, but then the words kept streaming out, louder than I meant them to and saying more than I wanted to say. "Her name was Mary Kate. She was a real person . . . for a little while, anyway." Now for sure I couldn't tell him about Miss Eliza. It didn't even seem like we were the same people anymore.

Bobby had stepped back when I started yelling, his black eyes wide.

"Sorry," I said. "I didn't mean to yell at you, it's just that everything's wrong. All the time."

Bobby put his hands in his pockets. "It's okay," he said. "I mean, not okay that the baby died, but it's okay that you yelled."

I nodded. I was still angry, but not at Bobby. And there didn't seem to be anything more to say. Bobby turned to leave and then stopped.

"What I came to tell you is that me and the Hendersons are building a dam. You know, down where the creek runs through the meadow. Across the road from the churchyard."

"The Henderson twins? Jimmy and Wayne?" I knew who they were, but since they were older—probably fourteen by now—I had never been around them much. "What about Caroline, Ruthie, and all your cousins?"

"Yeah, well, Jimmy said anyone could help. We're making a swimming hole. It's the best place for it, but that's Papaw's land, so they had to ask. We want to get it deep enough to jump into from the willow tree. You want to help?"

"Maybe," I said. But I wasn't sure. If it was just the

Millers, I might, but . . . Bobby was waiting for an answer. "I might come down later. I'll see."

"Okay, well, I'll be seeing you then." Bobby started down the driveway. Near the bottom, he turned to look at me. I lifted my hand. He waved back.

When I went inside, Grandma called from the kitchen. "Bobby didn't stay long."

"No," I answered. "He had to go home." I didn't want him to stay around here, but I couldn't tell Grandma that. I walked into the living room and stood there looking at Mama. I was invisible, for all she cared. How could I get her out of that chair? The heavy Shakespeare book was still lying on the floor. I picked it up.

"Mama, can we read the play together today? You said we were going to the Shakespeare Festival this month. We won't have time if we don't start reading it soon."

"I don't think so," Mama muttered.

"Can't you do *something* with me, Mama?" I set the book back on the floor next to her rocker. "We could take a walk. Let's see if the blackberries along the road are ripe enough to pick."

Picking blackberries on Tater Hill was always our favorite summer thing to do. We'd pick so many that we'd fill up all the containers Grandma could dig out of her cupboards. Then Grandma would pull out her huge canning pot and cook up jars and jars of blackberry jam. We always brought some home to Florida with us to give as gifts, but there was plenty left for us. Even when I ate blackberry jam on my toast on Christmas morning, it tasted like Tater Hill in the summertime.

"Let's go check on the blackberries," I repeated. *"Please?"*

Mama shook her head. I wanted to shake *her,* make her move out of that chair. But I had never done something like that to anyone, especially not a grown-up or my own mother. What could I do to wake her up? I looked around the living room and spotted Grandpa's hi-fi set. This time I'd put music on without asking first. And turn it up loud, so Mama couldn't shut it out.

I leafed through Grandpa's records, looking for something with a whole orchestra playing, not just a piano. Beethoven's Fifth Symphony. That would do it. No one could just sit quietly through an opening like that, least of all Mama, who loved music.

Careful not to scratch the record, I set the needle down and turned the volume up. Even I jumped when the music started. DA DA DA dum . . . DA DA DA dum . . . I looked at Mama, expecting her to sit up straighter and turn around. But all she did was curl up smaller, holding her head down in her lap and covering her ears with her hands.

Grandma came into the living room with a dish towel in her hands. "Annie, what's all this noise? Why so loud?"

I looked at Grandma, then back at Mama. "I . . . I was trying to get her to listen . . . I . . ." There was nothing more I could say, except sorry, but I wasn't really sorry. I lifted the needle and turned off the hi-fi.

Grandma was still watching me, and Mama still had her hands covering her ears. I slammed the front door on my way outside. Maybe that would make Mama notice that I was gone. I kicked a stone in the driveway, and it went flying into the side of the car.

Oh no. Clasping my hand across my mouth, I looked around, hoping no one had seen. Maybe I had done *too* much slamming and kicking. I went over to examine the car. There was a tiny dent in the faded blue paint, small enough that I thought no one would see. But when I stood up, I saw Grandpa pulling weeds in the garden.

He straightened up slowly, rubbing his back. "You must be very angry, Annie Annabel."

"It's Mama," I blurted out. "She won't talk to me. She won't do anything."

Grandpa sighed and said, "I know, I know." He paused to take off his cap and wipe the sweat from his forehead. "She's hurting, Annie. It takes time to work through the grief of losing the baby."

"We all lost the baby!"

"Yes, Annie." Grandpa was walking closer. "But she was the mother. That's hardest to bear."

"She's *my* mother, too, and I'm still here," I yelled back. "What about me? Aren't I good enough?"

I caught a glimpse of Grandpa's arms reaching out to me, but I didn't wait to hear what he had to say. I took off running. It was the only thing that seemed to get the sadness, and now the anger, out of me—that and the rock baby and Miss Eliza. Always before when something bad happened, Mama had been there to comfort me.

I slid most of the way down the path to the creek. Everything was still muddy and slick from the rain. As soon as I grabbed the rock baby from its resting place, I followed the other path up to Miss Eliza's house. By the time I reached the back door, I had used up my anger, but not my loneliness. Miss Eliza would listen to me and understand. I paused to catch my breath.

She was nowhere to be seen. The door was closed, and the banging sound was in full rhythm—bang swoosh bang, bang swoosh bang. I knocked several times before the banging stopped and I heard the tap of footsteps heading toward the door. Then there was silence.

"Miss Eliza, it's me, Annie. I mean, Annabel."

Another short pause. Then the lock clicked and the door opened. Miss Eliza looked small in the dark shadows of the room. Her eyes were squinted half-closed in the sudden light from the outdoors.

"I've come to help you take the boards off the windows," I said.

Miss Eliza wrung her hands together like she was squeezing out a wet washcloth. "I've been thinking I don't have a mind to do that quite yet, child."

"But you need light in your house, Miss Eliza. How can you see what you're doing?"

"I have my kerosene lamps, but . . ." She was silent while she considered what should be done. "I'll allow as how the house could use a tad bit of airing out, and I don't have close neighbors to be looking in. I reckon we could open up the side windows. Not the front of the house."

"That sounds good," I said, and followed her into the shadows of the room. Before my eyes adjusted to the dim light, the thick mushroom odor of dampness, mildew, and stale air hit me like a brick wall. It was all I could do to keep from going back outside for a gasp of fresh air, but I didn't want to hurt Miss Eliza's feelings. I stayed where I was, trying not to breathe in too deeply.

"We'll need some tools," Miss Eliza said as she rummaged through a closet tucked under a narrow stairway to the loft above. "I know I have a hammer, and I reckon this'll work." She pulled out a long iron rod, flattened at one end.

When she turned to look at me, she stopped for a second and said, "Oh, Annabel, I know my home is not fit for visiting. I've been here but a few short weeks, and there's much fixing to be done yet. You best wait outside whilst I find my hammer."

"It's okay," I said. "But . . . why do you live here?"

"My name is on the deed, child. And I needed a roof over my head." She went back to looking for her hammer.

Now that my eyes were accustomed to the dim light, I looked around. The worn floor shifted and creaked beneath my feet. It was sad to think this was the only place

Miss Eliza had to live. Maybe she was somehow related to the murderer, but I knew there was no way she could *be* the murderer. Not someone as kind and gentle as she was.

The sparse room was a combination kitchen and sitting area, but there was no refrigerator or electric stove. Not even a kitchen sink with a faucet. A bucket and wash pan rested on a long counter beneath the boarded-up window. Above the far end of the counter was a shelf with a few plates, some bowls, and one chipped china cup. A frying pan hung from a nail on the wall.

The cookstove with its two burners looked like a bigger version of the potbellied stove in Grandpa's workshop, but there was no cheery fire to chase the dampness from the house. A single kerosene lamp on the table in the center of the room cast a dim glow. The only other piece of furniture besides the ladder-back chair at the table was a sagging armchair, and a woven rug covered a portion of the rough floorboards.

"Where do you sleep?" I asked.

"In the far room." Miss Eliza pointed at the door to the other half of the house.

"Don't you have a bathroom?"

"No, child." Miss Eliza shook her head with a sad smile. "I'm blessed to have a home still standing after thirty years empty. The spring runs clear and I've a privy not twenty paces from the house. Enough questions now. I've found my hammer. We'd best get the boards down."

Back outside, I breathed in deep gulps of fresh air and carefully laid my rock baby on the back step. Then I followed Miss Eliza around the side of the house, where she was running her fingers over the rusted nails embedded in the boards.

"Grandpa pulls nails out with the hooked end of his hammer," I said. "I've seen him do that when he hammers a nail in crooked the first time."

"But there must be enough of the nail to hook on to, child."

"We could loosen the boards with the pole." I picked up the iron bar. It was heavier than I thought.

"I reckon we could pry the boards loose," Miss Eliza said. She took the bar from me and slid the flattened tip beneath the edge of one board. "I'll need a rock or a piece of wood to wedge in the space between the bar and the house. We'll use the bar as a lever."

I looked around for something the right size. Lying on the step was my rock baby—the perfect oblong shape—but there was no way I could use that. Instead, I picked up a short log from Miss Eliza's woodpile and wedged it into place.

It took the strength of both of us to force the board away from the window. Once the board started to give, we pushed the pole farther beneath it, and eventually the bottom pulled free. Then it was a matter of working the board back and forth enough to loosen the top end.

The first board was the hardest. But once we had our system worked out, the other three boards were down in half the time. Those on the north side of the house came down even quicker; they were half rotten and broke away after the first hard push of the lever. The back window was tougher because of the steep slope of the ground. I leaned from the edge of the top step, nearly losing my balance, while Miss Eliza stood below, stretched as tall as she could to reach the boards with the rod.

When the back and both side windows were clear, Miss Eliza stacked the boards next to her woodpile. "I'll cut them for firewood," she said, brushing her hands clean. "There's a bucket of springwater inside, Annabel. If you're as tuckered as I am, that water will taste right fine."

Yes, I was thirsty, too, and followed Miss Eliza back into her tiny house. We gulped the water down, me straight from the dipper and Miss Eliza from her chipped cup.

"Look at all the light in your kitchen, Miss Eliza."

"You're right, child, but now I can see the cobwebs floating in the corners and all else that wants fixing. I best give this house a good sweeping. And the window glass a soaping."

"Can we open the windows to let the air blow through?"

"If you like, child." Miss Eliza smiled.

Again it took both of us to push the windows up. One

was stuck closed, and we needed a stick to prop the other open. There were no screens, so flies and gnats and bees could sail in and out along with the crisp breeze. At least there would be clean air, I thought. It was already helping, or maybe I was getting used to the smell.

One more window remained to be opened, in the room behind the closed door. Without thinking to ask first, I pulled the door wide and expected to walk right in. But the small room was filled with a huge . . . *thingamajig*. I didn't know what it was. Maybe some kind of machine. It looked like something a kid would build with an Erector set, only much bigger and made of wood, with pedals near the floor, like a church organ. It was strung with yarn—yards and yards of it.

"Mind the loom," Miss Eliza said. "It's a bit close for a body to get round."

"Loom?" I asked. "A weaving loom? What do you make with it?"

"I weave coverlets and tablecloths, sometimes scarves and other yard goods. It's learning my mama passed on to me when I was young."

We inched around to the window. One pane was broken, and the frame was loose, but the light streamed in now that the shutter was gone.

Tight against the corner was a small bed, no larger than a cot. It was covered with a woven cloth in a pattern of interlocking circles, green on white.

"Did you weave that bedspread?" I asked.

"I did, long years past, when I was a girl," Miss Eliza said. "Would you like me to show you?"

She seated herself on the bench and left room for me to squeeze in the space next to her. "I work the treadles with my feet and slide the shuttle across the warp threads. Like this. Then I pack the weft threads into place with the beater."

Miss Eliza speeded up the pace of her weaving until it took on a regular rhythm. The stepping on the treadle, the swooshing of the shuttle being thrown across the warp, and then the louder banging of the beater bar, packing the weft into place—bang swoosh bang, bang swoosh bang. I smiled at the sound of the reassuring rhythm. So this was what the banging noise was. More like a step swoosh bang, now that I knew what made the sound. I watched a pattern emerge in a soft blue and cream-colored fabric.

Anyone who could make something this beautiful could never be a murderer.

Chapter Eight

When I walked up the driveway, I could see Grandpa sitting in the porch chair, smoking his pipe. Maybe he was waiting for me. He had cleaned up, changed his clothes, and combed his hair. His new beard was filling out, fuzzier and not so scruffy-looking now. He met me at the step and wrapped me in a hug. I liked the scent of his pipe tobacco, mixed with the clean smell of his flannel shirt, and I stayed there breathing it in.

"Feeling any better, Annie Annabel?" Grandpa asked.

I nodded, my mouth and nose still pressed against his shirt.

"Don't ever think you're not a very important part of this family. You know that, don't you?" He held me out at arm's length so I had to look up. "Hmmm?"

I nodded again and smiled. "Thanks, Grandpa."

"Good." He kissed the top of my head. "Now let's get some supper."

"There you two are," Grandma said when we walked into the kitchen. "Annie, will you set the table? Everything's nearly ready."

As I laid the knives and spoons on the right side of each plate and the forks and napkins opposite, I imagined how pretty a tablecloth, woven by Miss Eliza, of course, would look on the dinner table. A blue and white one would go nicely with Grandma's dishes.

When we were all seated, Grandpa carved the roast chicken, giving me a drumstick. Grandma started dishing up the potatoes and lima beans.

"None for me," Mama said.

"But Maggie, you have to start eating something," Grandma said. "You'll soon be nothing but skin and bones. Try just a few bites."

"I'm not hungry," Mama answered. "And I'm not a child." Then she pushed back her chair and left the table.

No one spoke. When I finally looked at Grandma, she was biting her lip and staring down at her plate. There were new lines, kind of like deep grooves, between her eyebrows that I hadn't noticed before. Grandpa reached over and patted her hand.

"What are we to do?" Grandma whispered. Grandpa just shook his head.

"I wish Daddy was here," I murmured. "He'd know what to do."

"There was a letter from Robert today," Grandma said. "Maggie just held it in her lap when I brought it in from the mailbox. Didn't make any move to open it."

A letter from Daddy? I knew part of it would be for me, too. Mama used to tear Daddy's letters open, read them to herself first and then out loud. He always wrote special messages to me and even to Grandma and Grandpa because he knew they liked to hear about foreign countries. *None of us will get to hear this one.* And that got me to thinking about the journal I was supposed to be writing in. I knew I needed to continue it tonight, but how could I tell Daddy that Mama was sinking farther and farther away from all of us?

We ate the rest of the meal in silence. I cleared the table without being asked, ready to do anything that would keep me away from the living room, where Mama was back to rocking in her chair. "Can I wash the dishes, Grandma?" I asked.

"Why Annie, thank you," Grandma said, and went to watch Walter Cronkite's evening news with Grandpa.

I soaped up the dishes, swishing the sponge back and forth, and thought about Miss Eliza weaving at her loom. Someone knocked at the door. I reached for a towel to dry my hands and went to answer it.

Bobby stood there. *Again.* This time he was holding a bucket of vegetables. "Mamaw sent these up. We got more from the garden than we can use."

"Who is it, Annie?" Grandma called from the living room.

"It's Bobby. He brought us vegetables from Mrs. Miller's garden."

"Oh, that's nice of her," Grandma said. "Tell Ruby thank you, won't you, Bobby? And I'll be sending black-berries down to her soon."

"Yes, ma'am," Bobby said as he followed me into the kitchen.

I stuck my hands back in the dishwater, since I didn't feel like looking at Bobby. I was still a little embarrassed after this afternoon and washing the dishes would keep my eyes on the sink. "Did you finish the dam?"

"No, it's not deep enough yet. It's gonna be a good swimming hole when we're done, though." Bobby took the vegetables out of the bucket, setting the tomatoes one at a time on the counter, but not being as careful with the squashes and cucumbers. "Hey, Annie, you know what the Henderson boys said?"

"What?"

"There's a ghost living in the murderer's house up the road."

The bowl I was washing slipped out of my hands and clanked against the sink. I picked it up and checked for cracks while I tried to make my voice sound calm. "What do you mean, a ghost?"

"Jimmy said his dad saw smoke coming out of the chimney when he drove by at night. Never in the daytime. And there's creepy noises from inside. But it's still boarded up, and it looks like it's empty."

"I wouldn't believe anything those Henderson boys told you, and you know there's no such thing as ghosts," I said. *Maybe helping Miss Eliza take the boards off the windows wasn't such a good idea.* Good thing I didn't tell Bobby about her. I knew Miss Eliza didn't want people to snoop around. Her tiny house was far enough up the mountain that not too many cars went by, but now people must be starting to notice.

"Yeah, well, Jimmy and Wayne said they were going to check it out tonight. They asked if I wanted to go along."

"Tonight," I said, a little too loudly. I tried to calm myself down. "You're not going, are you, Bobby? Besides, why do they always call it the murderer's house? It's just the McGee house."

"I told you the story before, remember? Papaw said ol' lady McGee killed her husband. Course, she wasn't so old back then, I guess. It was longer ago than most people round here remember. Papaw said the trial was a big thing when he was a young man."

"I don't believe it," I stated as firmly as I could.

Bobby looked surprised. "Why not?"

"I just don't believe it," I said in a quieter voice. "And I don't think you should go with them. You're not, are you?"

"Why should you care?" Bobby looked at me like I was crazy. "What's wrong with you, Annie?"

I started rinsing the dishes, refusing to answer.

"Annie?" Bobby said again.

I turned the faucet on stronger, louder.

"Well, I guess I'll go," Bobby said finally.

I didn't turn around until I was sure he had gone and I had rinsed the last of the dishes and stacked them in the drainer. Grandma was standing in the doorway.

"What was all that talk between you and Bobby? Sounded like you two were arguing."

"Oh, nothing." I picked up the dish towel to start drying and so I could hide the tears that were filling my eyes.

"Didn't sound like *nothing* to me," Grandma said. "Oh lordy," she sighed. "You need your friends, dear. We all need our friends." Then Grandma spotted the vegetables laid out on the counter. "Just look at what Ruby sent us. She knows I didn't plant squash this year, and I was telling her most of my tomatoes have that black rot around their stems. Now, Ruby Miller is a good friend."

And so is Bobby. At least he was a good friend. I didn't really know what was wrong between me and Bobby, but something had changed and it was probably my fault. I wasn't sure how to fix it. Everything in my life had changed. Maybe Miss Eliza was my only friend now, and what would happen to Miss Eliza if the Henderson boys went to her house tonight?

I couldn't settle down. Instead of watching television,

I went straight to my room, but it was too early to sleep. The black-and-white journal was lying on the bedside table, still looking shiny and new. No creased pages, no cross-outs or eraser smudges. Just the wood curl and the twig of baby's breath I had pressed into it and the one entry I had written. I picked it up to read. It was from the first week Mama and I were here in North Carolina this summer—back when everything was fun and happy, before Mary Kate.

June 16, 1963
Grandpa drove us all the way up Grandfather
Mountain today, and his station wagon was huffing
and puffing by the time we reached the top. Going
down was more like a roller coaster because there were
no safety railings on the edge of the road, and the
brakes were smoking. It looked like it wouldn't be too
hard to miss one of those hairpin curves and fly right
off the side and into those waves of blue mountains
that go on forever in the distance. Bobby came with us.
Even though he lives here in North Carolina, he said it
was the first time he had been up Grandfather
Mountain. Before, it was just a mountain he looked
at. There were a gift shop, picnic tables, and hiking
trails at the top, but the best part was the mile-high
swinging bridge. I always thought the signs meant the
mile-high bridge was 5,280 feet aboveground, but I
found out it's just that the altitude is one mile above

sea level up there. Grandpa said you'd only fall about
100 feet or so if the bridge broke, but it was still a long
way to fall. I was a little scared when the wind (and
Bobby) got it swinging. . . .

That day seemed like a hundred years ago now. I
picked up my pencil and wrote today's date–July 20,
1963. Where should I start? It had already been a whole
week since Mary Kate had been born and six days since
she had died. I wondered if I would keep on counting the
days and weeks that passed since my life changed. How
could I possibly write down everything? It had become *so
much more* than just what had happened. Even if we
couldn't have a new baby in the family, would we ever go
back to being the way we were before? I tried to think of
how to describe Mama now, but it was more like writing
about a stranger. Daddy would never believe me if he
couldn't see for himself how Mama wouldn't talk to me
and didn't even want to listen to music. If I put the words
down on paper, it would seem like that was the way it
would stay forever. Somehow I thought if I didn't write it
down, life would still have a chance of being normal
again.

I picked up the little wood shaving, not so much of a
curl now that it had been flattened, but it was the color of
strawberry blond hair and part of what should have been
Mary Kate's cradle. The twig of baby's breath was flat as
a pancake, but still held its color. Maybe if I put bits and

pieces like these into the journal, it would be as good as words—kind of like a scrapbook that told the story of my summer. Daddy wouldn't mind that, would he?

Before I could change my mind, I went out to the hallway and got the bottle of Elmer's glue from Grandpa's desk. Back in my room, I glued the wood curl and the baby's breath side by side on the same page, next to today's date. I was already thinking of other things I could add—a rock would be too big and heavy, but I could find a thin sliver of shiny mica from the creek bank and a long, leathery rhododendron leaf from the bush behind the twin tree. By the time the glue had dried and I closed my journal, I was sure Daddy wouldn't mind.

Now there was someone else I needed to worry about. *Miss Eliza.* Every few minutes I put my head close to the open window and listened for any unusual sounds. Were Bobby and the Henderson boys out there somewhere? At some point I fell asleep, and didn't wake up until the bright morning sun shined in my window.

It was Sunday, and Grandma was dressed for church. "We need to thank Pastor Crouse for giving us the grave site on such short notice," she said at breakfast. "We're not even members of his congregation, but I think we should go this morning." Grandma looked around the table, first at Mama, who continued to stir her coffee, then at Grandpa, who simply shook his head.

"Annie, you'll go with me, won't you?"

Grandma sounded so hopeful, I didn't have the heart to say no. "I guess so."

"Good. If you get dressed right now, I'll have time to braid your hair so it won't be such a flyaway mess."

I didn't much like Loggers Hollow Church. I had been there enough times to know I enjoyed the hymn singing, but once Pastor Crouse got going, he worked himself into a ranting rage. When he started pleading with people to come up and repent, I almost felt sorry for him. This morning I looked around the church, wondering if anyone was ready to repent and what they would say if they did go up to the front of the church. But no one stood up this morning or any other time when I had been there.

After church, Grandma stopped to talk to Pastor Crouse at the door and then three of the neighbor women. I knew they were talking about Mama and the baby when I heard Mrs. Coffey say, "Such a shame." I didn't want to hear anything more, so I walked away, looking for some of the Miller grandchildren until the name *McGee* caught my attention. I stopped right where I was, trying to overhear the conversation.

"That McGee woman is out of prison. I read about it in the paper."

"You don't say," the other woman answered. "Been so long ago, I'd nearly forgotten the story. Where's she living? That ol' house ain't fit for habitating."

"No one's seen hide nor hair of her, but there's been smoke from the chimney."

The subject changed, but I stood there, stunned. *Miss Eliza isn't the murderer. She can't be. They have it wrong.* I looked out across the road and past the meadow to the creek. Bobby was already down there, and I could see another boy with him. Maybe one of the Hendersons. They both wore shorts and waded up to their knees in the water, moving stones around.

"I'm going down to the creek, Grandma," I called. I *had* to find out what the boys had done last night.

"You run on home and change first, Annie," Grandma said.

Within fifteen minutes, I was down at the creek, wearing my shorts and a sleeveless shirt. Caroline was there, too, pulling her shoes and socks off. The other boy was Jimmy Henderson. His twin brother, Wayne, wasn't around.

"Hi," I said. Bobby barely looked at me.

Both Bobby and Jimmy were concentrating on building the dam. They didn't mention anything about the night before until Caroline said, "Bobby, tell Annie what you and Jimmy and Wayne did last night."

I was almost afraid to hear. "What?"

Bobby started to laugh, and I could tell he was showing off in front of Jimmy Henderson. "We snuck up to the McGee house round about eleven and painted *murderer* across the front door. And then we pushed over the outhouse." Bobby was laughing so hard, he dropped the rock he was holding and bent over double. Jimmy slapped him on the back and laughed along with him.

I clenched my fists and watched both of them. I might have expected it of the Henderson boys; I didn't even know them. But not Bobby. Without thinking, I stepped into the creek and swung out hard, hitting Bobby square in the shoulder and knocking him backward into the water. "She is not a murderer!" I screamed. "How could you do that?"

Bobby sat up, coughing and spurting water out of his mouth. Both Jimmy and Caroline stared at me.

"She is not a murderer!" I yelled again.

Then, before anything else could be said, I was out of the creek and running across the field. The road would be faster than through the woods, even if there were people still milling around the church. I glanced back once to see if Bobby or anyone was following. All three were still in the exact same positions, watching me. I had to slow down, but I kept moving, even with the pain stabbing at my side and my breath coming in uneven gasps.

When I rounded the last curve, I saw the red paint before I could read the word. It dripped from the letters like blood from a wound. *MUDERER*. They couldn't even spell *murderer* right! Stupid boys! I stood on the edge of the crooked porch, my chest heaving from both the running and the anger. Closing my eyes and taking deeper breaths, I tried to calm myself.

"Annabel."

I opened my eyes. Miss Eliza stood at the side of the house. Her droopy sunbonnet hid her face, and she gripped an iron bar in her hands.

"Oh, Miss Eliza," I cried out, running to her. "Are you okay?" I flung my arms around her, hugging her tightly, iron bar and all. "You're not really a murderer, are you?"

Chapter Nine

Miss Eliza drew in a deep breath. I felt her entire body tremble as she breathed the air back out. Then she rested her head against mine for a moment.

"You aren't a murderer, are you, Miss Eliza?" I asked again.

"Oh, child," she said in a tired voice, pulling herself away so she could look me in the face. "Not a murderer. But I'm 'shamed to say, I did kill a man."

I stiffened, still holding both of Miss Eliza's arms. "Was it your husband, like folks say?"

Miss Eliza nodded. "He was my husband, but so many years have passed, it's hard to think of him that way. Come, child. I'll tell you the truth so as you won't think worse of me than is fitting." Taking my hand, she guided me around the side of the house. She laid the iron bar on the ground and went to sit on the back stoop.

"No, not here," I said. "I'm too mad at those boys for what they did to your house. Let's go down to the creek."

I led the way along the steep slope of the path, looking back several times to be sure Miss Eliza was following. I dodged a clump of new mushrooms that I knew she'd want to harvest, and we both slowed to step over a tree trunk, freshly fallen across the trail. I didn't stop until I reached the V of the tree and lifted my rock baby from its place.

The high water from two days ago had receded, and the big flat rock was streaked with mud and partly covered with twigs and dried residue. I brushed a spot clean, big enough for both of us. Then I sat down with my legs crossed, cuddling my rock baby in front of me.

Instead of sitting next to me, Miss Eliza perched on a higher boulder with her skinny legs and old laced-up shoes dangling down from beneath the hem of her skirt. "These bones warn't made for sitting on the ground," she said.

I looked up at her and waited.

Miss Eliza took another deep breath, pushed her bonnet back off her head, and began. "My husband wasn't my choice. He was older. He'd been widowed once and wanted a body to cook and do for him. And it was Depression times. My daddy had to make do for five of us. I was oldest. He promised me to Jake McGee without my say."

"He didn't even ask you?" I knew without a doubt that Daddy would never do that to me.

"No, child, he didn't," Miss Eliza answered. "Times was different then. It warn't too bad at first, but Jake liked his drink. He and his cronies had a whiskey still. A place to make their own corn liquor. The remnants are not far up the creek from here. And he'd come home corned more times than not. Sometimes he didn't come home at all, and that was good.

"I think my daddy felt bad about what he did, though he never said. He'd come and look in on me. Brought my mama's old loom and set it up in my house so as I had a means to make a bit of money."

"The same one that's there now?" I asked.

"The same," Miss Eliza answered. "I reckon I was near happy, for a time. I could feel my baby growing and moving inside me. I wove a blanket to wrap my child in the day it was born. A receiving blanket is what it was called. A pale yellow only a shade different from the one you dropped outside my house the other day. And I made a promise to my baby that I'd care for it better than my mama or daddy ever did for me. Weaving and dreaming was most all I did those days."

I looked down at the rock baby in my arms, wishing more than ever that it was Mary Kate I held wrapped in the soft yellow flannel.

Miss Eliza continued. "When he was sober, Jake liked the sound of the loom and watching the progress I made on a blanket or a rug, whichever I was crafting. But there came a night Jake burst into the house more corned than usual. He was angry that I was sitting at my loom and not setting his supper on the table. He hit me. Hard. And I fell against the loom. My arms caught in the thread before I could push myself up and move away from him. He hit me again. I can still smell the foul corn liquor on his breath. It made me heave all over the rug I was weaving, and that made Jake even wilder."

I had been staring down at the rock baby as I listened. Somehow, I couldn't look Miss Eliza in the eyes. But now I stood up, balancing the rock baby in one hand, and settled myself on the boulder next to her.

"Isaiah was born that night. Too soon and much too small. When he breathed, it was ragged and hard. Like he couldn't catch his own breath." Miss Eliza wrapped her arm around my shoulder and pulled me close. "I held him through that long night until he grew cold in my arms and the midwife took him away."

"Was he wrapped in his yellow blanket?" I asked, feeling the sting of tears in my eyes.

"Yes, child, and buried in it." Miss Eliza ran her rough fingers across the rock baby in my lap.

"And the preacher read those words from the Book of Isaiah before you even named him," I added.

"You're right, child." Now Miss Eliza stopped talking and looked straight at me. "Do you want to hear more, Annabel?"

I nodded.

"Jake was beside himself, asking for forgiveness, doing small things he never did before. But I paid him no mind. Then he turned to his drink again and got angrier and wilder than ever. It got so I'd arm myself with my fry pan before he'd come in of a night. I don't rightly recall all of what happened that last time. Seems he dropped something when he went to come after me. He bent down and I hit him over the head with my fry pan. I thought just to slow him down so as I could get past him and out of the house. I'd made up my mind to go back to my family no matter what they thought."

Somewhere in the telling, Miss Eliza had lifted the rock baby and now held it in her own arms, swaying back and forth.

"Did you run past him and get home to your family?" I asked.

"I did, child. I told my daddy I wasn't leaving whenever Jake came to take me back. Only, he didn't come. Not for two days. I began to think I was free of him. Then late in the afternoon, just as the sun was sinking so pretty over the top of Tater Hill, lighting up the sky in shades of pink with a touch of orange, the county sheriff came to the house.

"He asked did I strike my husband. Without thinking, I answered yes. Seems Jake never got up off the floor after I hit him with my fry pan. Next thing I knew the sheriff was arresting me for the murder of Jake McGee."

"Oh, Miss Eliza," I said. "Didn't you tell them it wasn't your fault? He was hurting you."

"The law wasn't that simple, Annabel. And I began to think maybe it *was* my fault. After all, Jake had asked my forgiveness after Isaiah died. It wasn't till I paid him no mind that he took to drinking again."

"What happened when the sheriff arrested you?"

"He took me away right then and there. I did see my daddy and my one brother, Ethan, a few times after that, but it was the last I saw of my mountains till a few short weeks ago. I remember at the time it was early spring. Birds had been singing and chirping of a morning. The trees had that haze of first green about them. Buds fairly bursting with the promise of leaves and life."

"But wasn't there a trial?" I asked. "Grandma and Grandpa watch *Perry Mason* every Saturday night. Perry Mason is a lawyer, and he has a detective who helps him find the guilty criminal so that the innocent person goes free."

"Oh, there was a trial, child. I don't know about this Perry Mason you're talking about, but there wasn't a criminal to find. I was the only one. I did have a lawyer, a right nice young man, Mr. Clint Hageman. I was his first case, and he pleaded self-defense on my behalf. But I had no bruises or injuries to be seen, only deep inside of me. And Jake McGee had good friends about these parts. My daddy's testimony and mine held no weight against theirs. The jury found me guilty and sentenced me to thirty years."

"Thirty years!" I gasped. That was almost three times as long as I had lived! How could anyone be cooped up in a prison that long and still be alive? "What did you do for all those years?"

"It warn't so bad after the first year or so. I was safe there. I kept to myself and learned to read. I hadn't much schooling before the Great Depression set in. I was needed to work the farm and watch the young'uns whilst my daddy sought odd jobs wherever he could. My mama had died young after Lizbeth, the youngest, was born.

"Once I could read, that made all the difference. There was a retired spinster teacher, Miss Priscilla Gibson, who would come once a week and teach the women. She took a liking to me, and before long she had me running the prison library. I read every book I could get my hands on, some more than once. Miss Gibson would bring in books she collected from the Woman's Club and church groups. I missed her once she passed on. After that, a local preacher's wife came, but all she brought for reading was the Bible. She insisted our minds be cleansed."

I thought about all those lonely years Miss Eliza spent in the prison and remembered what she had said after she recited the Annabel poem. It wasn't hard to memorize the words when she had "all the time in the world and naught else good to do with it."

Miss Eliza handed the rock baby back to me. "This stone does have a pleasing feel to it. I can see why you long to hold it," she said. "We best be getting up to the house. I don't trust those boys not to come back and do more harm."

"They wouldn't do that," I said, pushing myself off the boulder after Miss Eliza. "Not in the daylight, anyway. They're probably more scared of you than they'd let on. Bobby Miller told me there was a ghost in your house. It's your loom, you know. That step swoosh bang noise it makes."

"Well, I'd as soon have them keep right on thinking I'm a ghost, though I know that won't last long." Miss Eliza laughed. "You're wise beyond your years, Annabel, child. I'm proud to count you as my friend."

"But don't you have any other friends or family that could help you, Miss Eliza?" I had set my rock baby back in its resting place, and we headed up the path. "What about your family?"

"None that's kept up with me. I had word when my daddy passed on. My brother Ethan wrote letters about once a year for a time, but the last I heard he married and moved to the low country. There's one other I count as a friend, I reckon. It's the lawyer, Mr. Hageman, who felt guilty that he lost my case those many years ago. That good man kept my few belongings stored safe—my hog fiddle, the loom, my coverlets and such. He drove me here in his automobile when I was released. And he comes once a week on a Wednesday night to bring me eggs and milk and leftovers from his garden."

"Why Wednesdays?" I asked.

"His wife's night for choir practice." Miss Eliza chuckled. "She wouldn't hold with his helping an ex-convict, I reckon. He parks his automobile a bit up the road to Tater Hill, so as it won't draw notice, and he brings his hammer and nails to fix what he can in that hour he's here, though it's been but three weeks. I'd be hard-pressed to get by without his charity."

We were nearly at the top of the path. I had walked it so many times in the past week that I no longer had to catch my breath. Miss Eliza kept pace with me, the strings of her bonnet trailing from her hand.

It wasn't until I caught sight of the tiny house again that my anger at Bobby and the Henderson boys raged back, stronger than ever. "How will we scrape the paint off your door? And they didn't even know how to spell."

"Oh, the paint's no bother," Miss Eliza said. "Words hurt naught. Righting my privy is what worries me. That will take more than the strength of the two of us."

We walked the twenty or so feet to where the outhouse lay tossed on its side, the shallow pit exposed to the air.

Who can we get to help us? This was Sunday, so Mr. Hageman wouldn't come around until Wednesday night.

I wished Bobby was still the same Bobby he had been all the other summers I was here. I could have asked *that* Bobby to help, but not this one. Not the one who had helped tip over the outhouse in the first place, and not the one I had just pushed backward into the creek.

Chapter Ten

As soon as I walked into Grandma and Grandpa's house, the gloom settled over me. It was like something I could actually touch and breathe and taste, like invisible spiderwebs you walk through and can't pull off. No wonder I always wanted to be outside with my rock baby or at Miss Eliza's tiny, falling-down house. Inside here, I felt the way I used to when I was little and hid under my blankets after I'd done something wrong. It was suffocating, and I could only stay for a short time before I had to come up for air.

The window shades were lowered, blocking out the sun, even in Grandma's kitchen that was usually so bright. There was no sound—no one talking, no radio or music playing, no buzz of Grandpa's saw coming from his workshop. And some kind of food had burned in the oven.

In the living room, Mama appeared to be asleep in the rocking chair. I tiptoed into the kitchen and opened the refrigerator to reach for the milk.

"Where have you been all afternoon?" Grandma's voice startled me. I closed the refrigerator.

Grandma sat in the dining room end of the kitchen, her elbows resting on the table. She was holding a framed photograph in her hands.

"Are you okay?" I asked. Grandma never sat still, except when we were all at the table for dinner. She was always cooking, washing up, weeding the garden—doing something. Even when she watched television at night, she darned socks or mended clothes. Then I noticed that the table was still set for the big Sunday-afternoon dinner. No one had touched the plates. *Oh no, I forgot all about Sunday dinner.* "Grandma, are you okay?" I asked again.

"Absolutely not," she said. "No one ate any of the dinner I made. You never came when I called. Your grandfather took a load of rubbish off to the dump. And your mama"—Grandma lowered her voice, as if she couldn't bear to talk about Mama out loud—"wouldn't budge from her chair. Said she wasn't hungry." Grandma set the picture down on the table and rested her chin on her hands.

"I'm sorry, Grandma. I guess I forgot." When I hugged her, I noticed that her cheek was wet, and I could see that the picture she had been looking at was of Mama as a little girl. It was one of those tinted photographs, and her eyes were very blue. "How old was Mama when that was taken?" I asked in a small voice.

"She was about your age." Grandma wiped her hand across her cheek and gave me a quick pat on the arm. "I think it was taken around the time of her eleventh birthday. Wasn't she a pretty girl? I suppose, in the long run, it's best we don't know what lies ahead. I never would have thought she could be so sad."

Grandma pushed away from the table and stood up. "Oh, lordy, I'm getting old," she said with a sigh. "You must be hungry, Annie. Get washed up, and I'll put some meat loaf on the table. It can be your supper now. It's burnt to a crisp, mind you, and the potatoes dried out, but I'll not let them go to waste." She shooed me off toward the bathroom and reached for a hot pad.

The meat loaf *was* burnt and dried up like cardboard. It had never been one of my favorite meals anyway, and it was all I could do to chew it and then swallow without making a face. I took a big gulp of milk to help wash it down. The mashed potatoes were hot, but stiff. Only the scalloped corn tasted good.

Grandma stood there watching me for a minute, and then said, "Oh, Annie, I'm sorry, that meat's not fit even for the family dog. Here, give it to me." She took my plate and dumped it in the trash can. Then she took what was left in the pan and dumped it, too.

I couldn't believe Grandma had thrown all that food away. She always said that anyone who had lived through the Depression knew what it was to go without and never wasted good food.

"I'll make you a ham sandwich, dear," she said, already spreading mayonnaise on a slice of bread.

"What about you?" I asked. "Aren't you hungry, too, Grandma?"

"I expect I'll make another couple sandwiches once your grandpa sees fit to come home from his errands. And maybe I can get your mama to eat one, too."

When I finished the sandwich, I said, "That really *was* delicious, Grandma. I'm not just saying that, either. Do you want me to wash the dishes?"

"No thank you, dear," she said, laughing. "I need to stay busy." Grandma was looking more like herself again with her apron tied on. She stood at the counter, polishing her silverware one piece at a time. "Oh, by the way, your uncle Chris phoned this afternoon to check on your mama. He was hoping you'd be in to talk to him. He asked to be remembered to you."

"Uncle Chris!" He was my favorite uncle—actually, my *only* uncle—and he was young enough to be really fun when he was around. "Is he coming for a visit? That would make Mama happy, wouldn't it?"

"No, dear, I'm afraid not. He's got a heavy class schedule he's teaching this summer, and your mama wouldn't even talk to him on the phone."

"Oh," I groaned. Just another way in which Mama had changed.

Happy to escape to my room, I sat cross-legged in the middle of the bed and opened the big green book of American literature to page 764. Finally I had a chance to think about everything Miss Eliza had told me about her life. She *wasn't* a murderer, even if she had killed someone. It's funny how people can hear just one thing about someone and start telling other people until everyone thinks that's the *whole* truth. Miss Eliza's story was as sad as the beautiful Annabel Lee's. Maybe even sadder, because Miss Eliza had no one who loved her as much as the man in the poem loved Annabel Lee. Miss Eliza had no one to remember her when she was locked away in prison all those years. Someday I might write a poem about Miss Eliza's life. *Eliza McGee* had the same ring to it as *Annabel Lee*.

I skimmed over the first verse. Just for fun, I tried substituting some words. *It was many and many a year ago in a* . . . I had to think of something in place of *kingdom*. *House* . . . *road?* No, something with more than one syllable. *Cabin? Cottage?* Maybe *mountain.* I know: *Mountainside*

so high . . . clear? No, it had to rhyme with *Lee* or *McGee*.
Then I had it . . .

> *It was many and many a year ago*
> *On a mountainside so free*
> *That a maiden there lived whom you may know*
> *By the name of Eliza McGee.*

I looked around for something to write the verse
down on before I forgot any of the words. My journal was
lying on the bedside table where I'd left it the night before. It would work for a poem, as well as for a scrapbook.
I opened to a new page and started writing the verse, cen-
tered just like a *real* poem would be printed in a *real* book.

Then I went back to reading the next verse of the
poem out loud. A quick knock on the door stopped me.
Before I could say "Come in," the door opened and
Grandma stood there.

"I thought I heard you talking to someone, Annie."

"No, I was reading."

"Aloud?"

"Yes."

Grandma walked over to the bed and reached for the
book. "Why, that's your mama's college textbook. Poe's
'Annabel Lee'? I haven't read that for years and years.
What on earth made you pick out that poem?"

Not knowing how to answer, I finally said, "I like
the name."

"Of course you do, dear. It's a beautiful name—my own mother's name." Grandma smiled with a faraway look and then shook herself back to the present. "Well, I just came across Ruby Miller's pie plate and casserole dish that have been here full on a week now. I thought you might run them back down to the Millers' for me."

The Millers. I did not want to go anywhere near that Bobby Miller. Maybe he wouldn't still be at his grandparents' farm this late in the day. All I needed to do was knock on the door, hand the plates to old Mrs. Miller, and head straight back home.

The sun was still shining over the top of Loggers Knob, stretching its slanted rays into the hollow, when I trudged down the road to the Millers'. So much had happened during this long day, how could there be any sunlight left? I balanced both dishes in my arms. "It's not neighborly to send a borrowed plate back empty," Grandma had said as she spooned scalloped corn into the casserole dish. "You hold that upright, Annie."

When I saw Bobby playing tag with the other kids in the front yard, I stopped. Why couldn't it be just Caroline, Ruthie, or the other younger Miller grandchildren? Staying out of sight, I detoured around the side of the barn, behind the tractor and other farm equipment, and over to the Millers' back door to deliver the dishes.

Old Mrs. Miller was surprised to see me. "Why

Annie, the young'uns are all round front playing. Why don't you join them?"

I shrugged. Best not to say yes or no. "Grandma said to thank you for these," I said, handing over the dishes.

Now I had to get out of there before Bobby saw me. The kids' voices, with Bobby's ringing out louder than the others, were getting closer, like they were headed toward the barn. Had it just been earlier today that I had heard his stupid laugh as he bragged about what he and the Henderson boys had done? It made me sick just thinking about that red paint on Miss Eliza's door and the over-turned outhouse. Not the kind of sick feeling I could ignore—more like I was going to throw up. *Now*. A sour taste erupted into my mouth. I spit on the ground and looked around for an escape.

The rickety barn door sagged open. I slipped inside. It was dark and cool, but the air hung heavy with the scent of fresh hay. I stood still, waiting for my eyes to get used to the dim light. Finally, I could make out the bales of hay stacked high, nearly filling the big space of the barn that had been open for swinging on the rope barely a week before.

There were voices outside. "I thought I saw Annie." That was Caroline. Then Ruthie, "I know it was her." Last, unmistakably, Bobby, "Then she's got to be around here somewhere."

I did not want to be found. I could see much more clearly now. The bales of hay were like giant steps all the way to the ceiling at the back wall. I started climbing, toppling a bale as I hurried and scraping my knee against the coarse straw. I scrambled on, wishing for blue jeans and a long-sleeved shirt to protect my arms and legs from the scratchiness.

Near the top I discovered a hole between the bales where someone had not stacked them closely. Just as the door was swung wide with a squeak, sending a shaft of late sunlight straight up the center of the barn, I squatted inside the hole. Thousands of tiny wisps of hay floated on the thick air. I muffled a sneeze and kept my head down.

"Annie!" Caroline called. "Are you in here?"

"Why would she be hiding?" Ruthie asked.

"Who knows," Caroline said. "She's been doing dumb things lately, like pushing Bobby into the creek." She called again, "Annie!"

"She's not here." That was Bobby.

Then they were gone, pulling the door closed behind them. It was darker than ever, the only light visible through narrow chinks between the wall boards. I relaxed and settled in to wait until they forgot about me or figured I had gone home.

I couldn't believe I was actually hiding from Bobby. Even *hating* him now. Everything had changed so much in one week. Making friends had always been hard for me, since we had lived on so many different air force bases over the years. But when I did make friends, they were usually boys instead of girls. Mama said it was because I was such a tomboy. There was never any question about Bobby being my best friend here in North Carolina. Even though I was gone the rest of the year, every summer it was like I'd never been away.

This summer things had been a little different after Mama and I arrived and we were still looking forward to the baby. Even if Caroline hadn't told me, I would have known Bobby had a crush on me. And I thought maybe I had a crush on him. He was a lot taller this year and liked to show off how strong he was by swinging the smaller kids around and around in a circle, holding them by their arms. He swung me the most, even if I wasn't the lightest, and he would always hold on to me longer when he stopped, so I wouldn't fall over from dizziness. And then there was the day we all had a picnic by the creek, and he sat next to me. I decided to test it and moved to a rock that leaned out above the water. Bobby got up and came over to where I was. He said he liked my red hair. Only it wasn't red, he said. It was red gold, and he had lifted a long wavy strand. This new *mean* Bobby he had become didn't seem anything like the old Bobby.

I was getting itchy and feeling cramped in my hiding place. It was probably safe by now, so I stood up and stretched, then brushed the wisps of hay off my shorts and shirt and muffled another sneeze. I had started down the giant steps of hay when I saw him. Sitting on the bottom bale. Waiting.

I couldn't keep from gasping.

"I knew you were in here," Bobby said. "Caroline and Ruthie are still outside looking for you, but I heard you sneeze."

What could I say? If I wanted to get out, I had to climb past Bobby, almost shove him out of the way if he wouldn't move on his own.

"Why did you push me into the creek?" he asked.

I refused to answer.

"Why won't you talk to me?"

Shrugging, I climbed down the last few bales, concentrating on the bulky squares of hay instead of on Bobby. I reached the bottom one and turned to step down, but Bobby was right there, his face nearly even with mine when he was standing on the ground. He didn't budge.

For a second I stared into his face. Even in the dusky light of the barn, I could see his black eyes staring back. I moved to my left to go around, and he moved to his right, blocking me. I dodged right, but he was as fast.

Just as I had earlier when Bobby was standing in the creek, I thrust out my hands to push him. But this time he grabbed my wrists. I stiffened and turned my face away. Immediately, Bobby released my hands.

"Annie, why are you mad at me?"

"Because you go around painting *murderer* on doors and pushing over innocent people's outhouses."

Bobby jerked back a step as if I had actually spit at him. "What difference does that make? Maybe someone broke into it, but nobody lives in that run-down shack. Even if there was such a thing as a ghost, it wouldn't need an outhouse. The whole place is falling down on its own without any help from me and the Hendersons."

I stopped myself from flinging back words to defend Miss Eliza. The less Bobby knew, the better. "Well . . . if someone did live there, it would be mean." I knew it was a dumb answer, but it gave me a chance to move around him.

"Where are you running away to this time?" Bobby asked, his voice becoming singsongy.

"I'm going home."

"All you do is run away. Aw gee, Annie, aren't you ever gonna get over it?"

Bobby's words stung like salt water on an open sore. I looked at him. "Get over . . . it?"

I was at the door now, but something made me turn back. "For your information, someone *does* live in that little run-down shack. My best and only friend in the whole world. And we could use your help pushing her outhouse back up, since you knocked it over." I was running out of steam now, but I couldn't stop yet. "You'd better be there tomorrow morning to help us. And don't you dare tell anyone!"

Pushing open the barn door, I escaped into the blinding brightness of the sinking sun. I thought I heard Bobby say, "Annie, wait. I didn't mean it." But I wasn't about to stop.

Chapter Eleven

Running away *was* becoming a habit, I had to admit to myself. In a way, I wanted to stop just to show Bobby I wasn't doing exactly what he'd said I was. But his words burned into that empty hole inside me—the hole that nothing but my rock baby could fill. I'd cry if I slowed down and had to face someone right now. It would be worse if Bobby called me a cry baby runaway.

"Where were you?" Caroline said, appearing out of nowhere.

I stopped long enough to focus on Caroline. Ruthie

was right behind her. "I just—I had to take something to your grandmother." And I was off again.

Shadows fell across the road, and none of the last sunlight stretched into the woods. I stuck to the road long enough to get to the fastest, straightest path down to the V in the tree and my rock baby. I needed to hold it for a few minutes and then head back to Grandma and Grandpa's house before it got completely dark.

The woods were different in the dusk. There was none of the magical fairy-tale feeling with golden sunlight filtering in, lighting up patches of soft green moss or pointing out fallen tree trunks. It was more the scary fairy tale now. I was glad I knew the path so well—where to slow down because of slippery rocks and what logs or giant roots to jump over.

By the time I reached the V, my eyes were accustomed to the darkness—not that I could see *everything*. The rushing creek was an invisible sound, reminding me it was there even if I couldn't see it, and I tried not to think about the dark shadows that loomed. The rock baby lay in its place. I lifted it in front of me first, just like I would have if I was lifting a baby under its arms and looking into its face. Then I rested it over my heart, soaking in the weight and feel of it nestled against me.

My breathing slowed. The anger and hurt of Bobby's words slipped away. He was wrong. Even if I did run away too much, it was because I was running *to* something. And I knew I would never "get over" Mary Kate's death. Maybe it would get easier. Talking and thinking about Mary Kate was already helping, but that didn't mean I cared any less. Mary Kate would always be a real sister to me, even though I'd never seen her. She was a baby now in my mind, but in the years to come, I'd probably picture her growing older, learning to walk, saying her first words, and swinging on a swing that Grandpa would make for her. But no matter how much I imagined, I knew none of those things would ever come true. Mary Kate and I would never have any grown-up sister conversations.

What about Mama? What was she thinking while she rocked and rocked in that chair, staring at the empty fireplace? Mama would never "get over" losing Mary Kate, I knew. But would she get better? Would she ever be Mama again?

I squeezed my eyes shut, concentrating on my rock baby again for one last long minute. Then I tucked it back into the V. The woods were darker than ever now. More by memory than sight, I searched for the start of the path. Once I found it, I stepped carefully, focusing on the ground in front of me, not allowing those dark fairy-tale shadows to creep in and spook me.

Miss Eliza would be able to walk the path in the dark. What was she doing right now? Was she lonely? Maybe she was weaving at her loom in the dim light of her kerosene lamp, listening to the wooden sound of step swoosh bang. If she had books to read, Miss Eliza wouldn't be so alone. Story characters made good friends you could count on.

When I closed the front door behind me, Grandma called from the living room, "Is that you, Annie?"

"Yes." I stuck my head through the doorway. Grandma had a pile of clean socks in her lap, sorting them by color and rolling them into balled pairs.

Grandpa looked up from his newspaper and smiled. "I was about to turn the television on. It's *Bonanza* tonight, after *The Ed Sullivan Show*. Do you want to watch with us?" he asked.

I looked over at the back of Mama's head. Her messy hair hadn't been washed for a week, and Grandma's wool sweater was wrapped around her, the way it had been for days. It was almost like she had turned into one of those stone statues with the blank eyes. "I think I'll read in bed," I said. "I'm really tired."

Back in my bedroom I took my clothes off and dropped them in a heap on the floor. Pulling my nightgown over my head, I stretched my arms through the sleeves and crawled into bed. I balled my pillow up and hugged it to me. It felt okay, but it wasn't like my rock baby. I needed something heavy and solid.

What a long day it had been—it seemed more like three days. Had I done the right thing telling Bobby to help fix Miss Eliza's outhouse? Would he show up tomorrow morning? Even if he did, Miss Eliza might be scared of him. Or maybe she'd be so mad she wouldn't let him near her house. She might be mad at me for telling. And what would I do if I lost my only friend? I wished I could close my eyes and fall asleep, but the day kept running through my mind, like one of the home movies that Daddy showed us on the screen set up in our living room back in Florida.

How had Miss Eliza fallen asleep each night in prison for thirty years? Did she think about the sun setting over Tater Hill in the springtime?

Chapter Twelve

I woke up as tired as I had been the night before. Hoping to go back to sleep, I pulled the sheet over my head and closed my eyes. Then I remembered telling Bobby to meet me up at Miss Eliza's house. *Oh no!* I hadn't even told him what time. What if he got up there before I did? What would Miss Eliza think?

Rolling out of bed, I dug through my drawer for a clean shirt and put it on, along with my blue jeans. I looked in the mirror. My matted hair was still in loose braids, so I pulled the rubber bands off and worked my fingers through the long strands; then I brushed out the kinks and gathered my hair into a ponytail. *There, not so much like Pippi Longstocking.*

"I just want cereal for breakfast," I told Grandma in the kitchen. I glanced at the clock to see how late it was. Only a little after seven-thirty. I prayed Bobby wouldn't be up there this early.

Grandpa set his newspaper down and took a sip of his coffee. "You look like you're in a hurry this morning, Annie Annabel. Where are you off to?"

"Uh . . . I'm meeting Bobby."

"So you worked out whatever differences you had?" Grandma asked. "And what's this 'Annie Annabel' that Grandpa calls you now?"

Deciding to answer her second question and ignore the first, I said, "I asked Grandpa to call me Annabel, but he can't always remember to drop the Annie part." I glanced at Grandpa, and he smiled back at me. Then I filled my mouth with cereal so I wouldn't have to answer any more questions.

Once outside, I headed straight up the road to Miss Eliza's, but kept looking back to see if Bobby was coming. What was I worried about anyway? The *new* Bobby wouldn't show up to help.

Miss Eliza was sitting in her spot on the back stoop, strumming chords on her hog fiddle. She jumped when I said hi. "Sakes, child, you caught me unawares. It's early yet for you to be about."

"I had to come early, Miss Eliza. I had to get here before . . . well . . . Bobby Miller is one of the boys who tipped over your outhouse, and I told him he had to help fix it." I didn't dare stop talking before I had Miss Eliza convinced I had done the right thing. "He's not really that bad. I mean, he never would have done this before. And he thought no one lived here. I told you he thought there was a ghost—well, maybe not really a ghost, but I made him promise not to tell anyone you were . . ."

Miss Eliza put out her hand to touch my cheek, and I stopped in midsentence. "Don't fret yourself, child."

"But I didn't want to make you mad at me."

"Oh, Annabel." Miss Eliza shook her head with a little laugh. "No matter. 'Twas only a question of time till all the neighbor folk would know I'm here. And I knew afore I came home that most wouldn't welcome a woman such as me back to Loggers Hollow."

"But *I* like having you here. You're my only friend right now."

"Seems to me you have a friend in that Bobby Miller."

"Well." I thought about it. "I used to. But I *never* thought he'd do something as mean as what he and the Hendersons did to you."

"There's worse pranks. You make it right with your friend, now. I won't be the cause of hard feelings twixt the two of you." Miss Eliza stood up, holding her hog fiddle. "I'll set this inside, and then I reckon we should look at that privy of mine to see what can be done." When she came back outside, her floppy sunbonnet was tied on her head.

I had about given up on Bobby. Miss Eliza and I tried twice to lift the outhouse, but all we accomplished was to shift it farther off the pit. Plus, now two giant slivers were stuck in the palm of my right hand. Then I heard a "psssst, psssst" and my name being called out quietly. When I turned to look, there was Bobby standing up on the road, motioning to me.

"Annie, come up here," he called in a strained voice, like yelling in a whisper. His round eyes held big unspoken questions.

"No, you come here," I called back. "You need to help us. It's you and your friends who knocked it over."

"But . . ." Bobby raised his arms in a question.

"It's *okay*. Miss Eliza is not a ghost."

"I can *see* that," Bobby yelled back.

"And she's not a murderer!" I was getting angry again.

"If she's who I think she is, she killed her husband."

"In self-defense," I said.

Bobby stared down at me.

"Well, are you coming? Or are you chicken?" I challenged.

Bobby raised his arms again, this time in resignation. He started down from the road, making his way through the thick tangle of underbrush toward me, Miss Eliza, and the toppled outhouse. When he reached us, his knees were scratched from briars, and a long red line dripped down his legs to the top of his socks. He kept staring at me, sneaking side looks at Miss Eliza. His eyes still held questions. Now that his curly dark hair was falling forward into his eyes, he looked younger than he had the other day.

Bobby was bigger and older than me, and also bigger than Miss Eliza. I had always looked up to him, but for once I felt like I was in charge. "Miss Eliza, this is Bobby Miller. And he won't hurt you, I promise."

Miss Eliza nodded.

I glared at Bobby until he nodded back, but he did not look at Miss Eliza or put out his hand.

"You'll be in trouble for being up here, you know," he said in a whisper to me.

"No one will know unless you tell. And you'll get in trouble for what you did with the Hendersons."

"She's been in prison. She killed someone." He brushed his hair out of his eyes, still not looking at Miss Eliza.

"I know that, but you don't know the whole story. Miss Eliza's a good person, Bobby. And *her* baby died, too, right after he was born, just like Mary Kate."

Bobby's eyes widened. "Sorry," he mumbled.

"No harm, son," Miss Eliza said in her tired voice. "And long years have passed."

I took a deep breath. "We need to push the outhouse up, Bobby. I don't think it's really broken."

All three of us walked in a wide circle around the top-pled outhouse. The wood at the base was soft and rotted, so it had torn away easily.

"I guess we could just push it back up over the hole," Bobby said. "But I'm not sure it'll stay in place."

"We can bring back some of Grandpa's nails next time we come," I suggested.

"It'll take more than that to make it last," said Bobby. "There's nothing to hammer it to. Probably need to re-place some of those rotten boards."

"Best just get it up for now," Miss Eliza said. "Mr. Hageman can take a look come Wednesday evening. I wouldn't want you young'uns to be blamed for helping the likes of me."

The three of us huddled shoulder to shoulder, almost like we were playing a game. We braced ourselves against the slope of the ground and lifted the top of the small wooden building. It was a lot easier with Bobby helping. He really was strong. We managed to get the roof to shoulder height, but could push it no higher. Shifting it more to the left, we leaned it against the trunk of a nearby beech tree and then rested.

"You and your *friends* should have knocked it uphill instead of downhill," I said, digging at a new splinter in my finger. "It would have been much easier to fix it that way."

Bobby glared at me. "I didn't know . . . Oh, never mind."

Miss Eliza brushed a flap of her bonnet back from her face and looked at both of us with those soft gray eyes.

"Sorry," I muttered, more to Miss Eliza than to Bobby.

Bobby stood back and studied the tree that the outhouse was now propped against. "Maybe I could climb to that branch up there and scooch out far enough to slide my feet under the roof. I could lift from there, if you'd keep pushing from below."

"It's worth trying, son," Miss Eliza said.

With arms stretched upward, Bobby jumped for the lowest branch on the far side of the tree, pulled himself up into the fork of the trunk, then felt for another handhold. His wet sneaker slipped against the smooth, gray bark, and he grabbed a branch to keep from falling.

"Best come on down," Miss Eliza said. "I don't want more harm coming from this."

"No, I can do it," Bobby said. He inched around the wide trunk until he could get a good hold on another branch and then swung himself to the limb that stretched out in the direction of the outhouse. Holding on to a branch above and wrapping his legs around the limb that held him, he inched his way out till he could touch the roof with his foot. A little farther and he slid both feet beneath the overhang of the roof.

"Okay, I'm ready. You two push down there, and I'll shove the roof up with my feet."

On the first try, we got the outhouse almost to standing position, but Bobby couldn't stretch his legs quite far enough to push it into place. Miss Eliza and I lowered it back to the tree trunk, and Bobby inched himself farther out on the limb. It took four tries, but at last the outhouse was standing, though a little crooked.

Miss Eliza opened the door and stepped inside to test the steadiness. "A strong wind would topple it, but I reckon a body can use it. I'm beholden to both of you."

"No you're not, Miss Eliza," I said. "It shouldn't have been knocked over in the first place." I looked at Bobby, but I was no longer mad at him. He was the old Bobby again, and he had worked hard to fix what he had done.

Lifting my ponytail off my neck, I fanned my face with my other hand. I could see that Bobby was hot, too. His hair was plastered to his forehead and springing up all over his head. Dark sweat had soaked through his T-shirt. "Could we have some water, Miss Eliza? Please?"

"The air *is* close," Miss Eliza said. "Water would taste right fine." She led us the short distance back to her house, but hesitated on the back stoop.

I was sure Miss Eliza didn't want Bobby inside her house. Sinking down to the bottom step, I patted the space next to me. "We'll just wait here."

Miss Eliza slipped inside, leaving the door open a crack. There was still the faint mushroom odor and dank smell of a cave, but it was nowhere near as strong now that the windows were open. It would probably take forever to blow the smell clear after thirty years of being closed up.

Bobby whispered, "She really lives in that shack?"

"It's not so bad now that we have most of the boards off the windows," I said.

"You've been inside?" His eyes still spoke more than his words. "How did—?"

"Shhhh." I silenced him just as Miss Eliza opened the door, holding her chipped teacup in one hand and the long tin dipper in the other. Droplets of water dripped from the rounded end.

"I reckon you young'uns can share this," she said as she handed me the dipper.

"Thank you." I took a long drink. I could have gulped all the cold water down, it tasted so good, but I handed the dipper to Bobby to finish.

Miss Eliza sat on the top step above us and drank hers more slowly. Her cup looked like it had once been very special china, with its delicate blue pattern painted against the white.

"That's a pretty teacup," I said.

"Well, it was a fine one, long years ago." Miss Eliza smiled like she was remembering. "It's been used hard, but it was right special to my mama. She had a set of four cups and saucers, along with a teapot, a cream pitcher, and a sugar bowl. We drank from them once a week on Sunday afternoons when I was a child. My daddy let me take one cup and saucer with me when I left home. I reckon my younger sisters kept the rest once they grew up. They were young'uns, five and eight at the time I left."

Drops of sweat stood out on her nose, and a thin film shined across the top of her lip.

"Miss Eliza, aren't you hot? Why don't you take your bonnet off?" I asked. "Bobby and I are both sweating something awful."

"Oh, Annabel, child, I'd ruther keep it on." She ran the back of her hand across her upper lip and then wiped it on her skirt. "After years of confinement, I grow afeared of too much light, too much openness. It's comforting with walls close about me, even my bonnet sheltering my face."

"But how can you stand it?" Bobby blurted out. "Don't you want to get outside and breathe again? See all the things you missed when you were in ja . . ." His face flushed red.

I glared at him. "He didn't mean anything bad, Miss Eliza."

"No harm, child." Miss Eliza swept her bonnet back from her face and leaned forward. "You're right, son. I did have a yearning for the mountains, the clean sweep of meadow across Tater Hill. Craggy rocks offering a view of the world."

Miss Eliza stopped talking. She worked her mouth as if trying to get her lips around her thoughts and into words. "A body learns acceptance after a time," she finally said. "And acceptance becomes comfort and safety. I had my books. Reading and dreaming is what gave me the freedom to burst beyond those thick walls. It gave me the freedom to fly."

The fine, tissue-paper wrinkles on her face were smoother now and her gray eyes were bright. "You might not comprehend, but I'd have been right satisfied to live out my years in prison. I'd made a home for myself, running the library. The books were my kinfolk."

"And you have no books here, do you, Miss Eliza?" I said it more as a statement than a question. "Or family. Or friendly neighbors."

For the first time since Mary Kate had died, I felt something good surging through me. I knew what I had to do.

Chapter Thirteen

"Come on, Bobby." I was on my feet now.

Bobby stood up, but looked back when Miss Eliza said in her soft voice, "Now, Annabel, don't you go getting into harm's way on my account. Just leave it be."

"I won't get in trouble, Miss Eliza. And thanks for the water."

Bobby laid the tin dipper back on the stoop next to Miss Eliza. "Thank you, ma'am, and I'm sorry about . . . well, about what I did."

"No harm, son." When we walked around the side of

the house, Miss Eliza called after us, "You're good young'uns, both of you."

I trudged ahead, my mind whirling with ideas about what I could do to help Miss Eliza. Bobby quickened his steps to keep up with me.

"Where are you going?" he asked. "You're not telling folks we've been here, are you?"

"Course not. I've been coming here for a week now and not telling anyone." I stopped in the middle of the road and dug the toe of my sneaker into a crust of dried mud. "Thanks for helping," I said in a softer voice. "I wasn't sure you'd come after the way I yelled at you yesterday."

A car rounded the curve and swerved when the driver saw us. The horn blared. Bobby dragged me out of the road, and I caught sight of the face of a little boy in the backseat. He turned around and watched me out of the rear window until the car was gone around the next curve. The swirl of heavy dust settled on the road.

I waited a second to see if Bobby was going to say anything more about what had happened in the barn the day before, but it seemed like the moment had passed. I went back to thinking about Miss Eliza.

"More and more people will find out about Miss Eliza living in her little house, like those people who just drove by. But I don't want Grandma, *especially,* to know I've made friends with her. Grandma's not mean or anything, but she's . . . well, I can just hear her saying, 'You shouldn't be *associating* with someone who's been in prison.'"

Bobby laughed. "I know. Mamaw might not say the same thing, but there's lots of neighbor folk who won't . . . well . . . be neighborly. Miss Eliza's right nice, though. I liked her."

"She needs books. I've decided that's what she's missing most. I'm going to look through all the ones I have here with me, and maybe I can sneak some from Grandma and Grandpa's bookcase." I looked sideways at Bobby as we walked. "I never used to sneak around so much. But I'm sure Miss Eliza will take good care of the books, and I can put them back like they were never gone."

"There's the bookmobile, too," Bobby said. "You know, it parks in the Winn-Dixie parking lot every Saturday morning in the summer. Maybe I could use my library card when my mom buys her groceries."

"I never thought of that," I said.

We were even with the thick patch of blackberry bushes that grew just to the side of the road and covered the front of a rocky overhang, kind of like a shallow cave in the mountainside. Grandpa had once seen a black bear there, gorging itself on ripe berries. Whenever I passed it, I half expected to see another bear.

I glanced over there now and noticed all the berries, dark and plump, weighing down the branches. "Look, Bobby, blackberries." I started pulling them, popping some into my mouth and cupping more of them in my hands. "They're delicious. A little dusty from the road, but nice and juicy." I ate a few more.

Bobby helped himself, too. "If they're ripe here, that means they're ripe on Tater Hill."

"Let's go tell Grandma," I said. "Maybe we can go picking today. It's still early."

Grandma liked the idea of going to Tater Hill. "Oh, but what about Maggie?" she said, looking at Grandpa. "We can't leave her home by herself in the state she's in."

"Leave that to me, Katherine," Grandpa said, patting Grandma on the shoulder. "We simply won't give her that option. Now, you get your pots and berry-picking buckets out."

Grandma became all business, bustling around the kitchen, pulling containers out of cabinets. "Bobby, you'll go with us, of course. Run down to your grandmother's and bring back some of her buckets. I promised Ruby berries, too." Grandma opened the refrigerator and surveyed the contents. "Annie, I'll put together a picnic lunch, if you'll get all the containers into the back of the station wagon. And don't forget your straw hat. You know how easily you sunburn."

Less than an hour later we were ready to go. Grandpa brought Mama out of the house. Her hair hadn't been washed, but it was brushed and covered with a red kerchief. She still wore the loose, flowered maternity dress, but no wool sweater today. Even though Mama wasn't saying much, just seeing her move around outside made me feel better.

Grandpa settled Mama in the backseat next to the window. I went around the station wagon to the other door and slid into the middle. My shoulder brushed Mama's arm, and I held it there. I wanted to snuggle closer and lean my head against her, but for now just this little bit of closeness was good. Bobby sat on my other side.

We had to pass Miss Eliza's house before turning up the road to Tater Hill. I counted the curves in the winding road, preparing myself for the sight of the sad little house. Bobby nudged my knee and we both watched out the window. The red letters, splattered across the front door, glared back at us. Grandma looked twice and said, "What on earth . . . ?" But by then we were past the house and turning up the mountain.

The road didn't have a name, only an arrow on a post with the hand-painted words TO TATER HILL. The rains from last week had washed the dirt out so that it looked more like a rocky creek bed than a road. Grandpa maneuvered around the biggest rocks, but the two deep parallel ruts and muddy potholes tossed the car like it was a slow, jerky roller coaster. I hooked one arm through Mama's and was happy when she gripped back. With my other hand, I clung to the edge of the seat, trying not to bounce against Bobby. One big bump could bang our heads into the car roof.

The bottom of the car scraped across a rock and Grandma said, "Maybe we shouldn't try to drive up."

"It's not much farther," Grandpa said. "I don't want to give up yet."

The car labored even more slowly as we reached the steepest stretch. The old station wagon was going almost straight up, and I was afraid the slightest bump would send it somersaulting backward, end over end down the mountain. I held my breath until we rounded the last curve and caught sight of Tater Hill.

The road ended where a grassy field began. Grandpa parked the car right there, and Bobby and I piled out. The treeless meadow before us swept up and over the top of the mountain. An outcropping of rocks perched crooked on the northwest side, like a lopsided crown on top of the potato head.

"Can we run to the top before we start picking?" I asked. Bobby was already on his way.

"Wait, wait!" Grandma called. "I need help with all these containers. Drop some off at the blackberry bushes on your way up, please."

I returned to the car and grabbed an assortment of buckets and bowls, stacked inside each other. Wading through knee-high grass, I faced into the brisk breeze with my ponytail streaming out behind. The wind was one of my favorite things about Tater Hill. It was always blowing across the mountaintop, reminding me where I was. And Mama was here, too.

Wild blackberry bushes grew in a thick, prickly cluster

that separated the woods from the open meadow. They were protected from the strong winds, but away from the heavy shade of the trees. Sun poured down on me, and I soaked up energy that had been drained away the day before. Stopping long enough to set the containers on the ground, I picked a few of the closest berries. They were fat and juicy, sweet enough but with a bit of tartness still. Grandma said those made the best jam and pies.

The taste that was so much a part of Tater Hill was still on my lips when I reached the jagged rocks at the top. Bobby balanced on the highest point like a flagpole marking the summit, but I settled into a natural seat of stone and looked out at the view. Mountains rippled outward to the north and west in waves and waves of fading blue until they blended into the sky. *I'm on top of the world.* Somehow being here made me feel stronger.

Behind me were closer, greener mountaintops and a little valley with a farm nestled into the crease of hillside and hollow. A red tractor that looked the size of a toy inched its way across a striped field. Could that be the farm Miss Eliza grew up on? The one with a view of the sun setting over Tater Hill?

When I looked back down at the blackberry patch, Grandma and Grandpa were bent over the bushes. Mama wasn't helping, but she was sitting nearby on a quilt spread out on the grass. "We'd better go down and start picking," I said to Bobby.

"Race you," Bobby shouted, already leaping off the

rocks and sprinting through the tall grass. I was close behind, gaining more and more momentum the farther
down the hill I flew. But it didn't matter who won. I felt
wild and free, like a horse galloping down the open slope
of a hill.

By the time we reached the bottom, I was out of
breath and laughing. Mama looked at me and smiled. *Actually smiled at me!*

I pulled a handful of berries from the nearest bush and
handed them to her. "They're delicious. Taste them."

"Okay, you two rascals get to berry picking. We could
use your help," Grandma said to Bobby and me. She was
smiling, and Grandpa winked. We were all happy for
once.

We must have picked for an hour. I lost track of time.
Each of us took a section of bushes and moved steadily
along, trying not to miss a single berry. Halfway through
my section, I remembered my straw hat and got it from
the car. It was probably too late—my nose was already
feeling sunburned. I turned to gaze up at the crown of
rocks on top of Tater Hill, stretching out my arms and
arching my back. Mama was no longer sitting on the quilt.
It scared me at first, but then I saw her slowly wading
through the tall grass, making her way up the steep hill
toward the top.

"Look, Grandma," I said. "Mama's walking to the top.
I'm going with her." I took off, not waiting for an answer,
and called out, "Mama, wait for me."

She turned around and reached her hands out. We wrapped up together in a big hug until Mama started to topple backward, and we both sat down hard on the ground.

At first I thought Mama was hurt, but then she said, "Pull me up." Her tired face looked like she had forgotten how to grin, but she was trying, and that was enough for now.

"I'll pull you all the way to the top of Tater Hill, Mama. Or I can push, so you don't have to work so hard." And that was how we made it up to the rocky crown at the top.

Mama settled into the stone seat with a loud sigh. I snuggled in next to her.

"I've missed you, Annie," she said in a whisper.

"I missed you, too," I whispered back, "and Daddy."

"Daddy will be home from Germany in a few more weeks, and he'll drive up here to the mountains to get us," Mama continued. "We'll all be home before school starts. In no time, it'll be like we never left."

But what about Mary Kate? We won't have her. I was afraid to say the baby's name out loud. Would it make Mama cry again? I pictured the crib in my bedroom at home. Before we left for North Carolina, Mama and Daddy had rearranged my room to make space for the crib and a changing table. "The baby won't be sleeping in here for the first few months," Mama had said. "We'll wait until he or she sleeps through the night." But I had wanted the baby there right from the beginning.

"Are you ready for sixth grade?" Mama was asking. "It'll be a pretty big change for you, a much bigger school, but you've always been a good student."

"Switching classes for each subject will be different. I guess I'll like it."

Another silence. It was almost like Mama was learning how to talk to me all over again, but she didn't want to mention what was most on our minds. At least she was talking. I leaned in closer, and Mama slipped her arm around my shoulders.

A fresh gust of wind reminded me of where we were, and I turned my thoughts to the view in front of us. "The valley looks like one of Grandma's patchwork quilts, doesn't it, Mama? Squares of all different greens and browns. And look, even a silvery-blue thread of river running through it."

"That would be in Tennessee, I think," Mama said. "You know you can see into three states from this one spot. North Carolina, of course, and Tennessee out there to the west."

"And Virginia to the north," I added. "Too bad there aren't black map lines marking where one state ends and the other begins."

Close in to the south, edging out around the base of Loggers Knob, was the town of Dansboro. Each year more buildings and houses inched farther out into the valley.

"I can see the main street of town down there and the college campus," I said. "And isn't that the hospital?"

Wishing I had Grandpa's binoculars, I stood up to get a better look. Yes, it was the hospital, all right. That square building with the plain red bricks. In an instant I was back inside that empty waiting room, sitting on the sticky vinyl furniture next to Grandpa, waiting and waiting for some news of Mama and the baby. I could almost smell the leftover cigarette smoke that hung over the room and mixed with the doctor's office scents of antiseptic and Band-Aids.

At the long, low sound of a groan, I turned around, and there was Mama, huddled into herself the way she had been in the rocking chair every day for the last week. Just like someone had waved a wand and the light in her eyes had flickered out.

"Mama, what's wrong? What happened?" It looked like she was hiding from something. Her hands were covering her face.

"Mama." I tried again. "Talk to me, Mama." I hovered over her, rubbing her shoulders to warm her, trying to get her to sit up again.

She mumbled something.

"What did you say?"

"It's too hard. Just too hard . . ." And she was silent again.

"Oh, Mama, please get up." I looked down at Grandma and Grandpa and Bobby way at the bottom of the hill. I waved my arms wildly, trying to get their attention, but they were all busy picking.

"Mama, I'm going to get Grandpa," I said, and bent down to hug her. "Don't go anywhere. Please."

I leapt off the rocks and sprinted through the tall grass, just as I had earlier, faster and faster down the steep hill, trying not to stumble and roll head over heels. Where was that wild happiness of racing Bobby down the hill? I kept my eyes on the small bent figures of Grandma and Grandpa, picking blackberries.

Chapter Fourteen

I was breathing too hard to speak when I reached the blackberry patch. Grandpa looked up with a smile on his face. His fingertips were purple.

"Well, Annie Annabel, you're out of breath. Did you get your fill of the view from the top?"

I shook my head and tried to take a deep breath before speaking. "It's Mama. She was okay. She was smiling and talking. . . ."

"Yes?" Grandpa said. His smile was gone, and he set the pail of blackberries on the ground.

Taking a couple more breaths to steady my voice, I went on, "But then something happened. So fast. We were looking down at the town, and we saw the hospital. . . ."

"And . . . ?" Grandpa urged me on.

"She just changed. Her whole face. Like she went away somewhere." My voice was trembling again, and I bit my lip to keep it from shaking.

Grandpa had his arm around me now, and I looked down at his purple-tipped fingers. Grandma still hadn't spoken, but I knew she had stopped picking blackberries.

"Katherine," Grandpa said to Grandma. "We simply can't wait any longer."

I looked up in time to see Grandma nod. Tears were forming at the corners of her eyes, big wet globs that would overflow any second.

"There are medicines now." Grandpa dropped his arm from my shoulder and walked over to Grandma. He gripped both her clenched hands and lifted them, looking into her eyes. "It doesn't necessarily mean hospitalization or—"

"Don't say it," Grandma interrupted. "I can't bear to hear it said aloud."

"It doesn't necessarily mean that," Grandpa repeated. "But we must do something."

"What?" I asked. "What do you mean? Does Mama have to go back to the hospital?"

"It's not for you to worry about, Annie," Grandma said. She pulled her hands away from Grandpa and swiped her hand across her face. Her fingers were purple, too, and now she had a purple stain on her cheek.

"But I am worried!"

Grandma didn't answer. Tears slipped freely down her face now, and she reached for berries, one after another without even lifting her head. "I had hoped being out here today would help her," Grandma mumbled. "Oh, Maggie, Maggie, don't make us do it."

Do what? Why wouldn't anyone talk to me; tell me what I needed to know? What would happen to Mama? It couldn't be any worse than the way things were already, could it? I looked over at Bobby, but he had moved farther off, his face turned away, as if he shouldn't be part of something this personal.

Grandpa started up the steep hill. Then he stopped. "Bobby," he said. "I may need your help, son. Will you come with me?"

Bobby turned around. "Yes, sir." He looked over at me, almost like he was saying he was sorry. Then he followed Grandpa, whose head and shoulders were bent more than ever.

Halfway up, they stopped while Grandpa took his cap off and wiped the sweat from his forehead. Then he put his cap back on and they continued.

I couldn't watch any longer. Turning my back to the hill, I reached into the prickly branches and started grabbing berries. Faster and faster, squishing them as I pulled them from the branches and threw them into the bucket. Who cared if they were smashed or bruised? They'd soon be simmering away to nothing but juice and seeds in Grandma's big pot, anyway. The thorns jabbed my fingers and scraped across the backs of my hands. A trickle of blood mingled with the purple juice. I didn't stop. The pain on my hands kept my mind off the pain in my heart.

I filled two buckets before Grandpa and Bobby reached the car with Mama half-dragged, half-carried between them. They stopped several times along the way, and I stole glances at their progress. From a distance Bobby looked as tall as Grandpa.

Now Grandpa and Bobby lowered Mama to the quilt that was still spread on the ground. She wrapped one ragged edge around her, as if she were cold on this hot summer day. Grandpa leaned against the car. Bobby flopped down in the tall grass and rested his head on his knees.

After putting my two buckets in the car, I sat down next to Bobby. Now that he had been pulled into helping with Mama, it was like he was part of the family. I didn't say anything, because what was there to say? But I did lean in close enough to touch his shoulder.

Grandma had stopped picking, too, but was slower to walk over. I could see she looked everywhere but at Mama, sitting huddled on the quilt.

After some long moments of no one speaking, Grandma broke the silence. "I expect none of us has an appetite for the picnic lunch. Let's just go home."

I helped Grandma settle the containers of blackberries into the back of the station wagon. I figured all the time we spent situating them would be for nothing. As soon as the car started bouncing over the bumpy road down the mountain, the blackberries would spill out.

Grandpa and Bobby pulled Mama up without any help from her. It would have made more sense to roll her over in the quilt and pull her up by the ends. How could she change so quickly from being nearly her old self to something no more alive than a sack of potatoes?

While Grandpa tucked Mama back in the car, Grandma lifted the quilt from the ground, shook it out, and spread it over the containers of blackberries. I slid in one side of the car, and Bobby sat on the other side with Mama curled on the seat between us. We drove back down the bumpy road, with Bobby and me doing our best to keep ourselves and Mama from bouncing off the seats. Still, no one had a said a word by the time we reached the house.

Bobby helped Grandpa get Mama out of the car and then retrieved his buckets of berries from the back of the station wagon. He half-waved to me and headed down the driveway like he couldn't get away fast enough, but I didn't blame him. I couldn't stand to watch any more of Mama being lifted or carried or dragged around like a limp doll, either.

I slipped into my room, grabbed whatever books were closest, including the big green volume with all of Edgar Allan Poe's poems, and headed for Miss Eliza's house.

* * *

I stayed there for at least two hours talking to Miss Eliza about the books, trying to keep from thinking about what was happening at home with Mama.

"This is my favorite," I said, handing her *The Witch of Blackbird Pond*. "Hannah, the so-called witch, makes me think of you—just a little. Oh." I clasped my hand over my mouth. "I didn't mean to say you're a witch. Hannah isn't a witch, she's just . . . alone."

Miss Eliza chuckled. "No offense taken, child."

"And here's *Calico Captive*. It's another story of Colonial America. I know they're kids' books, but you'll like them. They're good."

"Oh, Annabel." Miss Eliza seemed to struggle for words, and I thought she might cry, except that her face looked happier than I had ever seen it. "I'm blessed," she said at last. "Every book is a blessing, and I'm blessed to have you."

"I saved the best one till last." With a magician's flourish, I handed her the big green textbook. "Ta-da! This one has all of Edgar Allan Poe's poems and stories. It's over a thousand pages long and has hundreds of things by other authors, too."

It was late afternoon by the time I returned home, and Grandma hadn't even noticed that I'd been gone.

The house smelled like sweet blackberries. I glanced into the living room. The rocking chair was empty. A simmering, bubbly sound drew me to the kitchen. Grandma stood in front of the stove, stirring slowly while she stared into the huge, inky pot. Rows of sparkling clean jars lined the countertop.

"Smells good," I said, sidling up to her.

Grandma jumped. "Oh, Annie, I didn't see you. Have you been here long?"

"No." I shook my head. "Where's Grandpa?" I didn't dare ask where Mama was.

"Can you spread that cheesecloth over the other pot, so I can strain the seeds out?"

I unfolded the gauzy white cloth and laid it over an empty pot on the other burner. "Where's Grandpa?" I asked again.

"Step back, Annie. This is hot. I don't want to burn you." Grandma thrust her hands into two thick mitts and lifted the pot from the stove. The steaming, thick blackberry concoction slurped over the side of one pot into the other, almost taking the cheesecloth with it. Before it could be pulled completely into the pot, I grabbed a corner of the cloth and held it in place.

"Thank you, dear," Grandma said. "This is the hardest part of jam making." She set the empty pot back on the stove and took the edges of the cheesecloth from me. "You can scrape out what's left in the other pot once it cools down."

I wasn't sure I wanted any. Somehow the thick purple remnants of jam didn't look as appetizing as I remembered. It smelled too sweet.

Grandma lifted the cheesecloth from the pot, heavy with seeds and now dyed a deep purple. She rolled it into a ball and tossed it in the trash can. "Not worth saving that."

"Grandma, where's Grandpa?" I asked a third time, silently adding *and Mama*.

Rinsing her hands under the faucet, Grandma turned to face me. "He's taken your mama to the doctor. I just don't know what to think. They've been gone hours now." She glanced up at the clock on the wall while she dried her hands on her apron. "I've got to ladle this jam into the jars before it sets. Then I'll seal them with paraffin."

In an instant Grandma was back to concentrating on the jam. It was like she had closed a door, and I was left standing outside. Couldn't the jam wait? What about Mama?

Already Grandma had dipped her giant ladle in the pot and spooned some jam into the first of the jars. A trail spilled over the edge and onto the counter with every spoonful. It wasn't like Grandma not to stop and clean it up. I waited another minute to see if she would notice, but she kept right on dipping. Soon there would be as much jam on the counter as there was in the jars.

I couldn't watch any longer. I escaped outside, shading my eyes from the bright sun. Beads of sweat were already forming on my forehead. I walked around the back of the house to my swing, wishing Bobby hadn't left. Finally I wandered to the end of the driveway, but there was no sign or sound of any approaching cars.

Sweet Williams, daisies, and blue bachelor's buttons

were growing in the ditch along the side of the road. I decided to pick a pretty bouquet I could give Mama when she and Grandpa got home. And if Mama didn't notice them, I would take them down to Mary Kate's grave.

By the time I had gathered as many flowers as I could hold, Grandpa's old station wagon rounded the curve in a halo of red dust. Mama was with him.

Chapter Fifteen

Grandpa slowed the car as he turned into the driveway. Before daring to look at Mama, I focused on Grandpa through the open window and searched his eyes. He winked, and a rush of hope filled me. *Maybe the doctor did help Mama after all.* I held up her bouquet and smiled. Mama didn't smile back, but she did look at me and gave a little nod. I raced up the steep gravel driveway behind the car.

Out of breath and bouncing on my feet, I waited for Mama to open her door. Grandpa got out and said, "How about giving your Mama some room to breathe, Annie Annabel. Don't overwhelm her."

"Did the doctor . . . ?" I couldn't finish my question.

"The doctor gave her some medicine to try, but . . ." Grandpa shrugged. "It won't be a miracle. He said to give it some time, and we'll see." Grandpa closed his door and walked around to Mama's side. "Why don't you go tell Grandma we're home? I need to speak with her for a bit."

I slipped another look at Mama through the open window. She was facing straight ahead, not making any move to get out of the car. *There is more they don't want me to hear.* I threw my bouquet of flowers to the ground and headed into the house.

"They're home," I called to Grandma.

"I see." Grandma was already walking into the entry hall, wiping her hands on her apron. She gave a big sigh, as if preparing herself for what was to come. "You could start cleaning up the pots and pans for me while I get your mama settled."

Clean up all that blackberry gunk? I opened my mouth to protest.

Before any words came out, Grandma added, "I know it's a mess, but . . . please, Annie. This is a very difficult time."

Of course it's a difficult time. Didn't Grandma know how hard it was for me, too? Or didn't I count? We'd already lost Mary Kate, Daddy was overseas, and now Mama was slipping away a little more each day.

Grandma must have been reading my mind, because

suddenly she pulled me into a tight hug. "It's a lot to ask, I know. But I'm counting on you, dear. I'll be in to help you as soon as I can."

I hugged her back. "Okay, Grandma." In the kitchen, I looked at the mess. Again I wished Bobby were around to keep me company.

Heat hung like a curtain of steam, as if the blackberry jam were still simmering on the stove. The sweet smell was sickening, and my shoes stuck to the floor.

Grandpa had said there would be no miracles. Mama wouldn't get better overnight, and the medicine might not work at all. But it had to help. Wasn't that what medicine did? When I had strep throat and a high fever, the medicine helped in a matter of hours. When my finger had been infected, the medicine helped by the next day. Of course, the doctor had given me a shot both times to get the medicine right in. And then I had continued with pills. Maybe Mama should have started with a shot.

The next morning Mama was not sitting in the rocking chair. I hoped I'd find her at the breakfast table. But no, only Grandma was in the kitchen, sitting at the table with her coffee and the newspaper.

"How about a bowl of cereal this morning?" Grandma said. "I'm cooked out after yesterday. And my back aches from bending over the berry bushes."

"Okay." Cereal was fine with me. I looked in the cupboard, pulled out the box of Rice Krispies, and got the milk bottle from the refrigerator. "Is Mama up yet?" I was afraid to ask if she was any better.

Grandma shook her head. "Still sound asleep when I peeked in her door. But sleep is a good healer."

I ate my cereal while looking at the cute little cartoony guys on the back of the box and listening to their snap, crackle, and pop in my bowl. It sounded almost as loud as the crunching of each bite I took. I stopped chewing and let the cereal and milk slide silently down my throat.

Jars of blackberry jam were still lined up in rows on the countertop. Yesterday afternoon I had moved them to the table and wiped the spilled jam off the counter. My fingers had been so jam-covered that I'd pressed a black-berry handprint on a page in my journal before I washed my hands—another day to tell Daddy about.

Then I started scrubbing. The smell of Comet cleanser and cooked blackberries mixed up together just about made me throw up.

When all my scrubbing had still not erased the stains from the pale green Formica, I wiped off the jars and set them back up, one by one, covering up the worst of the spots. Forty-seven jars I had counted—one less than four dozen. I wondered if Grandma had counted them. Would she miss one jar if I slipped it out of the house? Even if I was sick of blackberry jam, it would be a real treat for Miss Eliza.

I was wishing my pocket was big enough to hide a jam jar, when Grandma looked at me as if reading my mind again. I could feel my face turning red.

"Would you help me carry the jam out to the shelves in the garage, dear?" Grandma said. "I don't have room to store them in the kitchen."

"Sure." I couldn't believe my luck. As soon as I'd drained the last of the milk from my bowl, I set it in the sink and headed back to my room to change into my overalls—the ones that were loose and had huge pockets.

By the time I returned to the kitchen, Grandma had taken one load to the garage already. She had another four or five jars cradled in her arms, but I could safely manage only three at a time. Dropping one would make another huge mess to clean up, and I wanted to avoid any more slopped blackberries. I wasn't sure if I'd ever eat jam or even fresh berries again after these past two days.

"I think I'll stay outside," I said after the last trip to the garage.

"Are you going down to the Millers' to play?" Grandma asked.

I was silent for a second. If I said no, Grandma would want to know where else I was going.

"I might," I answered, and closed the door before more could be said. "Might" left it open, so I wasn't lying.

The jar fit easily into my side pocket, but bounced against my leg as I walked. At least my hands were free to grab branches and other handholds on my way down the steep path. First I headed for the V and my rock baby. I had not held it at all yesterday, and I was missing the familiar weight and feel that was becoming so much a part of my life. Even though I trusted Bobby again, I wasn't sure he'd understand about the rock baby.

Not wasting time at the creek, I just picked up the rock baby, nestled it into the front bib of my overalls like a baby kangaroo in a pouch, and headed on to Miss Eliza's, the other necessary part of my new life.

Miss Eliza sat on the back stoop with books scattered around the steps at her feet. The big green volume of American literature lay open in her lap. For once her bonnet was not hiding her head, and the silvery sheen of her hair was soft around her face, looking like it had been freshly washed. She smiled when she looked up at me and raised the book.

"This is medicine, child, medicine for my soul. How did you know?" Then she read aloud, "I heard the trailing garments of the Night . . ."

Slipping the rock baby out of the bib of my overalls, I perched on the lower step to listen to the words of the poem with the rock baby cuddled in my arms. The bulky jam jar forced me to stand again, and I pulled it from my pocket, setting it carefully next to Miss Eliza.

It wasn't until we both breathed in a short silence, while the last poetic words seemed to hang in the air, that Miss Eliza noticed the jam. Grandma had labeled the jar with the words BLACKBERRY, JULY 22, '63 scribbled across a piece of masking tape. "Oh, Annabel, another gift. I'm beholden to you and your'n."

"Grandma doesn't know, Miss Eliza. She won't miss

one jar, and no one misses me right now." I looked down at the rock baby, thinking about how different my life had become. Mama always used to know exactly where I was.

"Something more than grieving over your baby sister is gnawing at you, child. What is it?"

I tried to put my thoughts into words. "I guess it's Mama . . . I guess I'm just plain scared that she'll never be the same again. I mean, the way she always was before Mary Kate."

Even though Miss Eliza didn't say anything right away, I could tell she was listening. She had a softness to her eyes when she looked at me, and she didn't turn away or try to change the subject. Then she closed her eyes and nodded, and I knew she understood.

"The doctor gave Mama some medicine that might help, but if it doesn't, there's something else that scares Grandma. Something really bad, and she won't tell me what it is. I keep wondering how things could get any worse."

"Oh, Annabel," Miss Eliza began, and then stopped. She seemed to be choosing her words before speaking, and I hoped she wouldn't decide to be like Grandma and not trust me to understand. "Child, this manner of sickness is hard. There's no recipe to follow. It's more like feeling your way, and I reckon that's what your grandma is doing. Your mama is *her* baby, and she's afeared she can't help her."

"Yes," I said, and I thought about how Grandma had been holding the picture of Mama in her hands. "But it's more than that. Something that Grandma said she can't even bear to say aloud."

"Child, you're wanting the truth, even if it hurts some." Miss Eliza didn't ask it like a question, but she looked at me for an answer.

I nodded.

"In my experience there's nothing worse than the unknown. Once you know, you can ready yourself." She paused for a second and then said right out, "I reckon it's electric shock treatment that has your grandma afeared, Annabel."

"Electric shock?" My entire body gasped like I had touched an electric wire myself. "But how could that help anyone?" I was standing now, clutching my rock baby hard into my chest, so that it felt like the stone it really was—heavy and lifeless. In my mind, lightning flashed out of the sky.

"Annabel, child." Miss Eliza tugged at my arm, pulling me back down to the step and slipping her arm around me. "My intent was not to give you more fear. It's a treatment, something to jolt her back to reality, but only if other means don't work. Though there's more to it than that, I reckon."

"How do you know?" My voice sounded small, even to me. Could Miss Eliza have been through something like this, too?

"Oh, child, the prison is a hard place with hard circumstance, though not all bad. There was a woman when

I'd been there round twenty years. She spoke to no one and turned within herself, shutting out the world."

"Like Mama," I whispered.

"Well, it went on a long while, till she was taken to the hospital for a few days. When she returned, I'll allow that she was better. Course I didn't know her afore, but she talked and ate and would come by the library, regular as a clock."

"Was she your friend, Miss Eliza?"

"Of a sort, I reckon. She liked to read, so we had that in common. Now, don't fret yourself over this, Annabel. I told you so as you'd know the doctor would try it only to make your mama better. He may just decide to put her in the hospital for a time and try some other medicines."

I nodded, not wanting to move away from Miss Eliza's arm.

"And as far as your grandma not telling you, child— she's protecting you, too, though she might not comprehend that your imagination is worse than knowing the truth. More than likely she's keeping on with the ever'day sort of things so as she won't give in to the fretting and the crying. It's a body's way of coping. Otherwise it will drag you down so as you might not ever stop."

I looked at Miss Eliza. Yes, I could see that was what Grandma was doing. But was Miss Eliza telling me about herself as much as she was telling me about Grandma?

At any rate, Miss Eliza did have a way of making things seem not quite so bad.

Chapter Sixteen

"Could I stay here and watch you weave?"

"You're welcome to stay, child, though I won't be weaving this day," Miss Eliza said. "I completed the double rose coverlet."

"What will you do with it?"

"Mr. Hageman reckons there might be a buyer at a craft shop out on the big state highway. He brought me new thread. Cones of it." Miss Eliza's face lit up with the change of subject. "A bold red color, greens in all the shades of the leaves in the woods, and more of the natural cream. I best be dressing the loom again, preparing it for the next piece to be woven. It's an arduous process."

Miss Eliza stood as she spoke, brushed off her skirt, and picked up one of the books. "I detested warping as a young'un, but my mama said the more care a body takes with the warp, the easier the weaving task will be. I quite like it now, save for the bending and the concentrating, but it will take me more than a day. It's best done with two people."

I collected the rest of the books from the steps and followed her into the small house. It was dim inside, but fresher and cleaner than the last time I had been here. We laid the books on the table and went on to the crowded second room. The loom looked different empty, with none of the thick loops of warp thread or the beautifully patterned cloth that rolled around the cloth beam in front.

"Do you thread it like a sewing machine?" I was used to watching Mama change the thread, but I knew that took only a minute or two.

Miss Eliza chuckled. "I've not used a sewing machine, child. Though I've heard of their speed. This is the only machine I can work, other than my daddy's tractor and plow long years past. I reckon dressing or warping a loom calls for miles more thread, as we're weaving the cloth itself, not just piecing it."

At first I sat on the little cot and watched, but Miss Eliza soon had me counting and measuring the lengths of the threads. Then there was the chaining of the warp and the actual threading.

"My mama worked from the front, but I'd sooner start at the back," Miss Eliza said. She sat on the bench, bending over the loom, while I crawled down on the floor to help with the threading from back beam to front beam. Every thread had to pass through the little round heddle eyes of the four different harnesses. If I didn't concentrate on getting each thread right, it could mess up the whole piece of cloth being woven. The concentrating kept me from thinking and worrying about Mama.

Before I realized it, the morning was gone. We still weren't finished, but Miss Eliza straightened up, rubbing her lower back. "You best be getting home, Annabel child, or you'll be missed come mealtime."

I didn't want to leave, but I also didn't want questions from Grandma. "Can I leave my rock baby here, Miss Eliza, so I don't have to go all the way back down to the creek?"

Miss Eliza nodded. "You're always welcome. And since you've done much of the dressing of the loom yourself, it's only fitting for you to start the weaving of it. Would you like to learn, child?"

"Oh yes!" I couldn't believe she'd really let me do the weaving. "Will I be able to make something as beautiful as your coverlet?"

"In time, child. Best begin with a simple tabby. Then we'll move on to a sampler of more complicated weaves."

* * *

That morning started a pattern for my days over the next two weeks. As soon as I could finish any chores Grandma might set for me, I would slip away to my weaving lessons, giving Grandma the impression I was headed to the Millers'. I hoped Grandma wouldn't decide to pay a visit down there herself, but these days she wasn't leaving Mama alone. By noon I was home for lunch, and in the afternoons I'd usually meet up with Bobby to go back to Miss Eliza's.

Mr. Hageman had bought two gallons of white paint, and together Bobby and I painted the walls of Miss Eliza's kitchen. It was amazing how that one change lightened and brightened the little room. The old wood soaked the paint right up, and we had to put on three coats. I wished we could perk up the outside of the tiny house with fresh paint, too, but Miss Eliza was not ready for that. And I knew that something that obvious would call too much attention. People would notice Bobby and me there, and word would get back to Grandma real fast.

The day we finished painting the kitchen, Miss Eliza brought out her hog fiddle to celebrate. She started singing "Old Joe Clark," and before I knew it, Bobby got up and started dancing, right there in the tiny kitchen. The whole house got to shaking. He called it clogging, but Miss Eliza knew it as flat-footing. Whichever it was, it was fun to watch. I couldn't believe that was Bobby stomping and dragging and tapping his feet so fast like his knees would bend any which way. When he finished, he was red in the face. Not from being tired, but from being embarrassed when he looked at me.

"Why didn't you ever tell me you could dance like that?" I asked him.

He shrugged. "I thought you'd call me a hillbilly, you not being from around here."

Then Miss Eliza started in on "I've Been Working on the Railroad." We all knew the words to that. This time Bobby took two spoons from Miss Eliza's dishpan and played them on his knee, clicking away to the beat of the song. "Papaw taught me how," he said.

That was the best day of all. But each day a little more of my weaving sampler grew in front of the beater bar and wrapped around the cloth beam into a thicker roll of my favorite shade of green, first in a simple "over and under" tabby weave. When I was ready for something more complicated, Miss Eliza taught me a twill in several variations. It gave the cloth a pattern that looked like striped arrows. I would have liked to cut a piece of my sampler to put in my journal, but that would ruin it. A loop of the green thread would have to do instead.

I didn't have the speed or rhythm that Miss Eliza managed with her weaving. The hardest part was learning the feel of the treadles beneath my feet without stopping to look each time. Finally, I took off my shoes and counted the treadles out with my toes until I had them memorized. With each bang of the beater bar, hammering the weft into place, I felt stronger. Weaving was green cloth medicine to me, just like reading was Miss Eliza's medicine. It kept my mind from wandering and worrying.

Mama's medicine was working, too, a little each day, though it took more than a week to notice any change. She came to the table to eat now, and she showered and washed her hair. Grandma and Grandpa drove her into town to buy some clothes that fit. She wasn't completely the real Mama from before, but she was more than the thin shadow of herself, sinking into the rocking chair. She didn't laugh or smile, but she didn't cry, either. I took her hand once, and I wanted to squeeze it hard, even shake it to make sure it was real. But it was so thin, like paper stretched over the bones of a skeleton, I was afraid I'd break it as easily as I could snap a twig or crumble a leaf in my hand.

As long as Mama was moving and eating and talking, I told myself, there would be no electric shock treatment. And that was good.

Chapter Seventeen

On the morning of August seventh, I lay in bed, knowing that it was my birthday, of course, but thinking it would probably not be much different from any of the other days during the past few weeks. Oh, I knew Grandma was baking my favorite angel food cake with orange glaze drizzled over it, and there would probably be some presents. Bobby might come up to eat dinner with us. But Daddy wouldn't be home from Germany, and Mama wouldn't suddenly become her old self again. That much I knew for sure.

Something was different, though, and it wasn't just the smell of bacon. It was *sound*. Not the clanging of pans or an electric mixer buzzing away in the kitchen, but musical sounds. The house had been silent for weeks now, as if a cloud of red dust from the road had clogged our ears and throats. Even though Mama smiled once in a while, there was still no laughter or singing or music in the background, the way there always was when Daddy was home.

But yes, it was music. Not a record of Mama's favorite piano sonatas or a symphony orchestra. This was Grandpa's music. The tunes he'd waltzed to as a young man. The kind he had ice-skated to—once even with Helen Hayes before she became a famous actress.

Flinging back the covers, I didn't stop to get dressed or to grab my slippers from under the bed. I ran out to the living room, my nightgown fluttering around my ankles. Grandpa was leaning over the open hi-fi set, the jacket of the record album still in his hands.

"Grandpa, it *is* you."

He turned around, grinning. "I thought this house needed some waking up," he said. "May I have this dance, Annie Annabel? Miss Eleven-Year-Old?"

"Oh yes, Grandpa. Yes." I composed myself, held the skirt of my nightgown out as if it were a fancy ballgown, and curtsied.

Grandpa bowed low, reached out his right hand, and swept me into a waltz pose. He bent to my level, while I danced on my tiptoes. We'd done this before, though not in a long time. I knew the moves. Only Grandpa would dance with me like this, whirling around and around like those wonderful ballroom dancers in movies, where you could go on forever in joyous motion, forgetting everything.

But Grandpa was out of breath by the time the first selection ended. The second one began—one of those ragtime pieces with an uneven rhythm. Grandpa laughed. "Let me rest first before I can keep up with that one."

I kept twirling around on my own until I realized Grandma was standing in the doorway watching us with the first smile I had seen on her face for weeks. Had she been there the whole time? I was so caught up in waltzing with Grandpa that I hadn't noticed anything else.

"You two are quite the pair," Grandma said. "Your grandpa hasn't danced with me like that for years." She winked at me—or was it at Grandpa? Then she asked, "Is French toast and bacon okay for your birthday breakfast, dear?"

"Oh yes, please."

"Take a look over here, Annie Annabel," Grandpa said. He pointed to the corner next to the fireplace.

There stood a rocking chair—smaller than the one Mama always sat in, but not a little kid's size, either. Was it for me? It looked my size, with some growing room built in. The seat was a smooth gloss of newly varnished wood, and the back had an inset of woven cane where my head would rest. The rockers were thicker, heavier than most and a slightly different shape, as if they were meant for something else. Then I remembered my curl of a wood shaving from the floor of Grandpa's workshop.

"The cradle! You made this from . . ."

Grandpa nodded before I finished my sentence, and touched his finger to his lips. "I thought this was best made for you, Annie Annabel. You always like to watch me at my woodworking. And you would appreciate the labor of love."

I sat in the chair now, testing out the size and leaning my head against the slight give of the caned back. My arms rested on the sheen of reddish blond wood.

"I could have stained it a darker cherry, but the natural color seemed right for you," Grandpa said. "It will darken with age."

"Of course the natural cherry is right for Annie," Grandma said. "It's just the color of her hair."

"I love it, Grandpa. Thank you."

"What's all the commotion so early this morning?"

There was Mama standing in the doorway next to Grandma. She looked sleepy and her hair was rumpled, but she sounded like herself. My first thought was *We're a family again*. Only Daddy was missing, but he'd be home in another week. "Grandpa made me this rocker," I said. "Isn't it beautiful?"

"What's the occasion?" Mama asked.

We turned to her in surprise.

"It's . . . my birthday . . . Mama. I'm eleven today, remember?"

"No, it's not." Mama sounded so certain that I didn't know what to say.

"Maggie, of course it's Annie's birthday," Grandma said. "We discussed this yesterday, remember? I baked an angel food cake, and you watched me separate all the egg whites."

"Of course I remember the cake. But don't tell me I don't know my own daughter's birthday, and stop treating me like a sick child." Mama had backed into the hallway while she was speaking, and now she turned away to her bedroom, slamming the door.

No one spoke. After another pause in the music, the record launched into a faster piece where the instruments seemed to go in all different directions. I didn't think I could stand to listen to it. I went over to the record player and lifted the needle.

Grandpa had that old, tired look again. Grandma was still in the doorway with her hand to her cheek, as if she had been slapped. Her mouth was open in an O shape. She was going to cry, I knew it.

"Oh dear, I . . . I . . ." Grandma heaved a sigh and reached her hands out to me. "I just don't know what to say." She looked to Grandpa for help, and he stepped closer, wrapping both of us in a hug. That was better. I could keep my eyes closed, my head pressed between Grandma and Grandpa, and not think.

"It's the medicine, Annie. She's not herself. We all know that," Grandpa said. "Baby steps. That's what it takes. Little steps toward getting better."

I nodded, but couldn't say anything. *Baby* was not the word to use. Now all I could think of was the tiny *baby* grave Mary Kate was buried in. How could someone's mother not remember her birthday? Would Mama remember Mary Kate's birthday? Couldn't a mother love more than one child? I had never worried about being loved before. But that was before Mary Kate.

Grandma pulled herself away from the hug. "I'll start the French toast," she said. "You have some presents at your place at the table, dear." I felt Grandma's hand on my back for a second before she left the room. I knew she was trying to keep things normal, just the way Miss Eliza had said.

There were no more tears stored up behind my eyes. I wasn't going to cry. More than anything, I was worn out. It would be easier to go back to bed than to eat breakfast, but Grandpa was already propelling me toward the kitchen.

Three presents and an envelope sat next to my plate. Grandpa picked up a box. "Why don't you open this one first? Bobby brought it yesterday so you'd have it first thing this morning."

"Bobby did?" I was surprised he hadn't waited until he saw me later in the day. I tugged at the Scotch tape, trying not to tear the paper.

"It's okay to rip it off," Grandpa said.

Yes, ripping would be good. I was tired of tiptoeing and doing everything so carefully, not making too much noise, not bothering people, having to sneak off to Miss Eliza's whenever I could. I tore the paper off in two swipes and opened the box. Then there was more paper, wrapped around the fragile legs of a china horse, posed with one hoof lifted and its leg curved as if in the midst of a trot. This paper I pulled off gently. The horse was a chestnut, the color I would have chosen if I could have had a real horse of my own. Bobby must have been thinking of my birthday last year. I had used my ten dollars of birthday money to pay for one hour of horseback riding lessons. I paid for Bobby, too, so I'd have company.

"Why, that was very thoughtful of Bobby," Grandma said.

It was hard for me to smile, but I tried. "Yes, it's really nice." I *did* think it was beautiful, and I knew the exact place I'd put it on my shelf back home, where I had a whole collection of china horses. While I was here in North Carolina, I'd keep it on the bedside table next to the journal.

"The mail's from your daddy," Grandma said. "It arrived yesterday. I wondered how he had managed to time it just right for your birthday."

At least Daddy didn't forget. I looked at the colorful foreign stamp before I tore the envelope open and pulled out a card. There was a picture of a dancing, round-faced, brown-eyed girl, wearing an apron over her dress and a kerchief on her head. Printed in a curve at the top of the card were German words: *"Haben Sie Alles Gute zum Geburtstag!"* On the inside, Daddy had written "Have a Happy Birthday." Underneath was a note.

> *Dear Annie,*
>
> *I'm sorry I'm not home for your birthday, but by the time you open this card, it will only be another week. You should see the mountains here in Germany! Some of them even have snow in the summertime. They're bigger than the mountains in North Carolina, but they make me think of you. I'm bringing your present with me. I know this is a sad time for everyone. Try to have fun on your birthday. I'm sending you a hug and a kiss, and give Mama a hug from me, too.*
>
> *Love, Daddy*

I closed my eyes and pressed the card to my chest. *Only another week.* I'd keep this on my bedside table as a reminder that Daddy was really coming back, and then I'd put it in my journal along with the other memories from the summer. Once Daddy was home, Mama had to be more like herself again—that is, if she could get through this week without needing electric shock treatment. Would electric shock make her memory better or would it make her forget even more things?

The next package was a blouse, white with tiny green

and blue flowers all over it. "Hold it up to you, Annie," Grandma said. "I thought it would go nicely with your navy blue jumper. Your mama and I picked it out when we were shopping this past week."

"Mama picked it out?" I asked. "She knew it was for my birthday?"

"Oh . . . well, yes." Grandma paused. "It's got to be this medicine making her forgetful, Annie. You know she couldn't really forget your birthday."

"I guess. . . . Thanks, Grandma. I like the blouse."

There was one more present. It was a book, I could tell by its shape, and I knew it had to be from Uncle Chris. Every single birthday he sent me a book, and he always picked a good one. It was wrapped in the brown paper it had been mailed in, and I was careful not to tear the book jacket as I opened the package. *A Wrinkle in Time* by Madeleine L'Engle. I hadn't heard of that author before, but as soon as I turned to the first chapter and read, "It was a dark and stormy night," I knew it was a book I could get lost in. And that was what I needed today.

"Why don't we give Uncle Chris a call?" Grandma said. "I know he'd love to hear from you."

"Yes, that would be good," I said. "Maybe a little later." I *would* like to talk to him, but not now. I didn't think I could talk to anyone else right now, not even Uncle Chris.

After breakfast, I asked Grandpa if he could carry my rocking chair back to my room.

"Don't you want it out here in the living room for watching television with us?" Grandpa asked.

"Maybe tonight, but right now I just want to sit in it while I read my book."

And that was where I spent the morning, not even budging from my chair, which Grandpa had wedged into the space in front of the window. A steady rain was falling outside, and every now and then thunder rumbled. I thought about Miss Eliza, who was probably expecting me for my weaving lesson. But she would understand if I didn't come when it was raining. And I knew she would understand that it was a good day for reading.

I was on page 113 when Grandma knocked. "Lunch is ready, Annie. You should take a break from your reading."

"Can I finish another chapter first?" I didn't want to sit at the table if Mama was there, too. What would I say to her? Would Mama still insist that it wasn't my birthday?

"Well, I've made you a sandwich," Grandma said. "Don't wait too long."

It was close to two-thirty when the rumblings in my stomach finally sent me out to the kitchen for my lunch. I was hoping no one else would be there so I could keep on reading, but Grandma was at the sink, peeling pota- toes. The rain was falling harder outside, and the radio was on. That made it easier for me to avoid having to talk. The *Swap Show* radio announcer rambled out a list of items that people wanted to swap for something else. "A washed pair of men's overhauls, only wore twice, no patches on the knees; three calico kittens, seven weeks old, no swap asked; 1958 washing machine, ringer in need of fixin' . . ."

Grandma laughed out loud. "What would someone trade for those?"

I tried to keep my mind in the fantasy world of *A Wrinkle in Time*. Meg Murry's life and fears made me stop thinking about my own. Calvin was as good a friend as Bobby, and Mrs. Who, Mrs. Which, and Mrs. Whatsit were the tiniest bit like Miss Eliza. Wackier, of course, but they cared about Meg and Charles Wallace.

"We interrupt this program for a special news report." The official-sounding voice drew my attention toward the radio, and Grandma reached over to turn the volume up.

"First Lady Jacqueline Kennedy has given birth by emergency caesarean section to a son, five and a half weeks premature, at Otis Air Force Base Hospital in Massachusetts at 12:52 p.m. today. The baby, weighing only four pounds, ten and a half ounces has been transferred to Children's Hospital in Boston for specialized treatment for breathing difficulty. Mrs. Kennedy is reported to be in good condition and recovering. The president was with his wife, but now has accompanied his newborn son to Boston. Mrs. Kennedy became the first American First Lady to give birth while her husband was in office since Mrs. Cleveland in . . ."

Grandma had gasped with the first words, and now she stood with both hands pressed to her chest. "Oh my," she said. "Oh my . . . the poor Kennedys."

I didn't know when I had gotten out of my chair, but here I was, standing next to Grandma. "Just like Mary Kate," I whispered.

The special news report was over, and now the *Swap Show* radio host was back on with his rambling list. Grandma switched the radio off. "Well, this baby will have the very best medical care in the country," Grandma said in a more normal voice. "I'm sure he'll be fine."

Would Mary Kate have been fine if she had better doctors in a big city hospital? I hadn't thought about that before. And how would Mama feel about this? Would she feel better if this little baby boy lived, even though Mary Kate hadn't?

Grandma was still talking as if she was trying to convince herself. "And of course the Kennedy baby is not *as* premature. Did they say five and a half weeks? He weighs a bit more than . . . Mary Kate."

That was the first time I had heard Grandma say "Mary Kate" out loud. It was always "the baby," *if* Grandma even talked about her. "Maybe we shouldn't tell Mama," I said. "Until we know what happens."

"Not tell me what?"

Chapter Eighteen

For the second time today, Mama had startled me by sneaking up to the doorway without a sound. "What shouldn't I be told?" she demanded.

I didn't know what to say. *Why is Mama so angry?*

"Maggie," Grandma began. "It's . . . it's nothing." She turned back to the potatoes in the sink.

"Obviously it isn't *nothing*, if my daughter doesn't think I should be told. I'm tired of being handled with kid gloves, or talked about as if I'm deaf." Mama glared at both of us.

"Now, don't take it out on Annie. We simply didn't want to open raw wounds," Grandma said. She moved away from the sink again and used her apron to dry her hands, even though they weren't wet. "It's the news report. The Kennedy baby was born early. A little boy. He's been taken to another hospital, a better one with facilities for premature infants."

"*No,*" Mama groaned. Suddenly she was hunched over, clutching at her stomach, the way she had for those long days in the rocking chair. "Not Mrs. Kennedy, too. This kind of thing doesn't happen to . . ." She didn't finish her sentence.

"Now, Maggie," Grandma said. "The baby is alive. The newsman said he had breathing difficulties, but I think he's expected to improve. I'm sure the Children's Hospital is the best there is."

"And Jackie? How is she?" Mama said it like Mrs. Kennedy was her best friend. But really, it was kind of like the whole country knew the president's family personally. They were always on the news or the covers of magazines. It was fun having a young president with kids living in the White House. I couldn't remember any pictures of old President Eisenhower and his family.

"Mrs. Kennedy had a caesarean section, but they said she was in good condition. She's still at the other hospital recovering," Grandma said.

"I'm turning the news on." Mama was already headed to the living room and the television set.

I didn't follow. I couldn't watch Mama like this anymore. Back in my room, I tried to get into the mood of my book again, but thoughts of the little Kennedy baby kept creeping in. If it hadn't been raining so hard, I'd have gone down to Miss Eliza's, where I kept my rock baby now. Holding it would help fill that hole that was deepening inside me again. *How is Mrs. Kennedy?* I wondered. *Did she get to hold her baby before they whisked him away?*

Mama didn't leave the living room for the rest of the day. Bobby came up for supper, and after I blew out the candles, we ate my birthday cake in front of the television—something Grandma usually didn't allow. The one good thing was that Mama didn't say it *wasn't* my birthday again.

The Kennedy baby was named Patrick Bouvier. Once that announcement was made, he seemed more real, stronger somehow. I thought that was a good thing. The news reports said he had something called hyaline membrane disease, which meant that his lungs weren't developed enough. It was the same thing the doctor had told Grandma and Grandpa about Mary Kate, only our doctor hadn't given it a name. Patrick was in a giant pressure chamber at the hospital in Boston, and the news had shown President Kennedy walking into the building without his usual smile or wave at the camera. Were Caroline and John Jr. being told anything about their little brother?

Of course, they were really little, but at least they had each other.

Before I went to bed that night, I got the Bible from the bookcase in the living room and found the verse from the Book of Isaiah that Miss Eliza had told me about. I read silently to myself, "He shall feed his flock like a shepherd. He shall gather the lambs with his arm, and carry them in his bosom, and gently lead those that are with young." I prayed that this little baby, Patrick Bouvier Kennedy, who shared a birthday with me, would be strong enough to breathe on his own.

He wasn't strong enough. Less than two days later, early on August ninth, Patrick died. When I got out of bed that morning, Grandma told me the news. The report had said that "the struggle of the baby to keep breathing was too much for his heart." *Even the president's baby couldn't be saved.* Mama's eyes were red and swollen all over again. Grandma cried, and even Grandpa wiped tears from his eyes. I wanted to cry, but I couldn't. I wondered if my tears were dried up forever.

Were the president and Mrs. Kennedy crying? I remembered how bad it was having the Millers stare at me after Mary Kate died. What would it be like for the president's family with the whole world feeling sorry for them and watching every time they came outside?

Throughout the long day between my birthday and when Patrick died, I dragged out the reading of *A Wrinkle in Time.* Whenever I really liked a book, I couldn't stop reading, but this time I didn't want it to end. I read each page twice, sometimes three times, before turning it. I felt like I knew the characters, and I wanted to keep them as my friends. Once I finished the book, they would be gone.

On the night of August eighth, I'd gone to bed with one more chapter left to read. The next morning, after I found out about the president's baby, I read the last chapter. Thank goodness it was a happy ending. I needed that. Meg Murry loved her little brother, Charles Wallace, so much that she was willing to risk her own life to save him, and it worked. I wished there had been some way for me to save Mary Kate's life, or even Patrick Kennedy's. What would Mary Kate have been like at Charles Wallace's age? Most likely she wouldn't have been a genius like him, but I was sure she would have been smart.

In the book when Meg, her father, and Charles Wallace finally came home, her mother and brothers raced outside to greet them and ended up in one great big hug with the entire family. That part hurt the most. In less than a week now, Daddy would come home, but when he did, would Mama get up from her rocking chair? And even if she did, would she always be angry and forget things? I finally closed the book and decided I wouldn't wait another minute before taking it to Miss Eliza.

Grandma was standing at the door, urging Mama to come outside with her to weed the flower bed along the edge of the driveway. "The sunshine will do you good,

Maggie. Maybe put a little color in your cheeks," Grandma said. "If you don't feel like working, just sit in a chair."

I didn't stay around to hear Mama's answer. Slipping out the back door, I took the overgrown steps that hardly anyone ever used to get down to the road. I was sweating before I reached the bottom. The rain had stopped the day before, but the air was *close,* as Miss Eliza would say—heavy and hazy, as if the sun were shining through a dirty window. Instead of walking up the road in the heat, I headed for the trail through the woods and skidded down the bank. The cool shade of the forest drew me into its greenness. It was like entering a different world, almost magical with the rays of sun filtering down through gaps in the trees like shafts you could actually touch.

Taking my time, I headed in the direction of Miss Eliza's house and stopped once to lie down on a soft pillow of moss. Then I was sidetracked by a cluster of orange touch-me-nots. I set my book down and ran around squeezing as many pods as I could. They burst open like tiny springs. Grandma called the flowers jewelweed, and the blossoms did look like bits of jewelry. I liked to think how many more little jewels would grow up next year because I'd helped spread the seeds.

When I finally reached the house, Miss Eliza was not home. I knocked and then opened the door to call inside. There was no answer, but I could see the hog fiddle on the kitchen table and the china teacup next to it. Setting the book on the table, I went back outside. The little house was looking more like a home inside and out, even though the front windows were still shuttered and the word *muderer* was still painted on the front door. But in the back, there was a thick green and yellow yarn rug on the stoop where Miss Eliza liked to sit, and a broom was propped against the wall.

Knowing Miss Eliza couldn't be far, I scanned the woods for a sign of her. I followed the tracings of a new path down a gentler slope than the one I had taken to get here and finally spotted the bonnet bobbing up and down as Miss Eliza bent to pick something from the ground and stood again. By the time I reached her, I could hear the loud rushing of the creek water, which meant the water-fall was close.

"I've brought you a new book," I called out. "I know you're going to like it."

Miss Eliza smiled. "I thank you, child, and I have two to return to you." She set her basket down. "I've missed you these past two days. I expect the rain kept you from coming for your weaving lesson."

"Yes," I said, even though it was more than the rain that had kept me away. I didn't want to talk about it now, though. "What's that you have in your basket? It's not just mushrooms this time."

"Some dandelion greens I came across in a sunny spot near the creek, and I decided to dig some sassafras for brewing tea."

I reached for the bare brown root in the basket and lifted it to my nose. "Mmmm, smells kind of like root beer. I didn't know you could make tea from this. Does it taste good?"

"Well, I reckon I'll try. My mama used to make it for us young'uns when we were feeling poorly."

"You're not feeling sick, are you, Miss Eliza?"

"Oh no, child," Miss Eliza chuckled. "Just varying my diet. Seeing what I can find to eat in these woods."

"Will you hike to the waterfall with me? It's not much farther."

"I reckon I could, Annabel. I've not ventured that far these past weeks I've been home."

The waterfall at Loggers Creek was more than just one fall. It was a series of small cascades, like an uneven staircase dropping and curving down to one final plunge, as high as a house was tall. Bobby and I weren't allowed to come here by ourselves, but at least once a year we talked someone, usually Uncle Chris when he was visiting, into hiking with us. The pool at the bottom made a wonderful wading pond, not deep enough for swimming, but great for cooling off up to our knees after the hike. Today it was deeper, though, full of runoff from the rain, and the sound was a constant roar of water swooshing over the top.

Miss Eliza and I walked to the edge of the water, our shoes making prints in the gravelly mud. The roar from above drowned out all other sounds, so we didn't try to talk. Miss Eliza gazed up at the falls and closed her eyes, catching the light spray of mist on her skin. *She looks so young.* For a minute I could picture exactly what she must have looked like as a girl. Had she come here with her brother and sisters, just as I did every year?

After a few minutes of enjoying the cool dampness, I decided to explore. "I'm going to climb to the top," I called out, though I wasn't sure Miss Eliza could hear me. I pointed to the rocks that bordered the falls, and Miss Eliza nodded and mouthed something. Probably "be careful." I was always careful here. I'd been warned often enough by Mama and Uncle Chris: "Don't get close to the edge."

The rocks were more like boulders in a giant ladder, steeper than my legs could stretch. Staying away from the wet, slippery ones, I climbed with hands and feet, fitting the toes of my sneakers into narrow crevices and reaching above my head for fingerholds to pull myself upward. It wasn't hard. I'd done this before, and each year was easier because I'd grown taller.

Halfway up, I stopped to rest and looked down at Miss Eliza. I waved and then stretched my arm up the next distance to feel for another handhold. My fingers slipped into a hole and before I could pull myself upward, a sudden stinging pain burned at my fingertips. I snatched my hand back, too stunned to yell or to understand what was happening. The burning sting didn't stop. It got worse, spreading over my entire hand. And then I knew what was happening. . . . *Yellow jackets!*

A stream of those ugly bees poured out of that hidden hole above my head and swarmed straight for my face! I screamed, trying to think. Trying to see how to get away. I could jump, *but where*? Into the waterfall? Down onto the other rocks? I couldn't even see anything now. Bees were everywhere—in my hair, on my forehead, in my ears, finding their way into my mouth every time I opened it. *Stinging, stinging, stinging* . . . Just as I was thinking that jumping into the waterfall would be better than this—*anything would be better than this*—I felt arms around me. Supporting me, pulling me backward down off the rocks.

Miss Eliza. I still couldn't hear anything but the roar of the water, or was it the buzzing of the bees in my ears? But the arms were Miss Eliza's holding me, sheltering me, helping me down from the boulders, pulling me up the path now, batting bees away from my face, pulling them from my hair.

My screams went on and on, or maybe I wasn't screaming now. Maybe it was someone else. I didn't know, but it felt like I was making a noise, each one ending in a hiccup I couldn't control. And my body felt like one huge, constant, burning *sting*. My throat was full of cotton. I was *so* thirsty.

We were almost up to the road now, and I could feel Miss Eliza's heaving body next to me, as if she couldn't catch her breath, either. But her arms were as strong as steel pulling me along.

We were at the road now, and Miss Eliza stopped long enough to push my hair out of my eyes. "We must . . . get you home, child. . . . You need . . . a doctor." Her voice sounded far away.

We started down the road in a slow loping run, Miss Eliza's arm around me, holding me up and keeping me going. It took forever. No cars came by. Why couldn't a car come and pick us up?

Finally I thought I saw the driveway. But everything was fuzzy. We were closer now—was that Bobby helping Miss Eliza pull me the last few steps? I could hear talking, but even the sound was fuzzy. Grandma was down on her knees in the flower patch, and Mama was sitting in a chair, staring at us.

Then I was in the car. Someone else had arms around me, propping me up. Was it Mama? A voice—Grandma's maybe—said, "Who is that woman?"

I tried to open my eyes, tried to see who she meant. It was like looking through a small crack in a board, but I could see Miss Eliza. *I think*. Where was Bobby? Miss Eliza was standing all alone, leaning forward trying to catch her breath, watching us drive away.

"Annie! Annie!" It was Mama's voice this time. "Talk to me, Annie. Don't go to sleep."

I tried to say I could hear her, but no words would come out. Everything was so slow. All . . . I wanted to do . . . was . . . sleep. . . .

Chapter Nineteen

"Annie, can you hear me? Try to open your eyes, dear."

It was dark. I couldn't see anything, and it was so much easier just to sleep.

"Listen to me, Annie. Please try to open your eyes. Just once, and then you can close them again."

Who is talking to me? The voice sounded familiar. A voice I heard all the time, so why didn't I know who it was? I'd think about it later.

Someone gripped my hand. Not too hard, but firmly pressing against each finger. "Annie, I need you to open your eyes and look at me. Please, dear."

I tried again, but it was like pulling magnets apart. Finally I kept them open long enough to see a light and a blank wall. I was lying in bed, but it wasn't my bed. And was that Mama? Mama sitting next to me and holding my hand? *Mama talking to me?*

"It's okay, Annie. Now you can go back to sleep for a while."

Was that *Mama*? *Smiling at me?*

The next time I woke up, it was easier to keep my eyes open, and there was light coming in a window. Where was I?

Bees! Swarming, swarming bees! The memory slammed back, and I jerked straight up, looking around. Where was I?

"Annie, it's okay, dear." Mama was standing there, right next to the bed, and now she leaned over to hug me. "It's okay. You're all right now. Just lie back and relax."

Sucking in a deep breath and letting it out slowly, I leaned back against the pillow. Mama smoothed my hair away from my eyes. I had so many questions, I couldn't think where to begin. But Mama seemed to know.

"You're in the hospital, Annie. The doctor wants to keep you here for a full twenty-four hours, just to make sure the poison is out of your system and you don't have another reaction." Mama's voice trembled, and she paused for a second. "Grandma and Grandpa were here with me through most of the night, until we knew you were safe. Then they went home to get some sleep. I couldn't leave."

"I thought . . . I thought I was going to die." My words came out stiff and hard, as if I hadn't spoken for a long time and something was wrong with my tongue. "I didn't even care. I just wanted to go to sleep forever . . . to make those bees stop . . . stinging me."

"I thought you were going to die, too," Mama whispered. She was holding both my hands now, gripping them together like hands in a prayer. "I was so scared. More frightened than I've ever been. I couldn't lose you, too, Annie. Losing a baby is terrible, something no one should have to go through, but"—she went on in a trembling voice—"but I couldn't lose the daughter I've loved for eleven years."

Loved for eleven years. So Mama did remember. I could feel a tremble run from her body straight through her hands into my own body—kind of like an electric shock.

"Your throat was nearly swollen shut by the time we got here," Mama said. "Your whole face was unrecognizable."

No wonder I felt so strange. I pulled one hand free and ran it over my cheeks.

"Yes, dear, you're still swollen. Your nose was flat across your face, and your eyes were little slits, like someone from outer space. You look better now, but you're still not yourself. Even your earlobes were huge." Mama shuddered again—another electric current—and was silent for a second. "And your hair. I'm afraid we'll have to cut away some of your beautiful hair. Bees are so twisted into it, I can't begin to pull a comb through the tangles."

"Bees in my hair?" I touched the snarled wads and pulled my hand away. *What if they are still alive?* "I don't care. Just get them out."

"They're dead by now," Mama said, laughing. "I think we can get away with just cutting a few inches. We'll see."

"Mama . . ." Now my voice was barely a squeak. "You're talking to me and laughing." I was almost afraid to say the words out loud. They might make Mama change again, the way she had changed so quickly before. I didn't care if they'd have to cut all my hair off, as long as I could keep Mama the way she was right now.

"Oh, Annie, I'm so sorry." Mama sat on the edge of the bed and gathered me up in her arms. "I know I've been locked away in some awful, lonely world, thinking only of myself. How could I forget that I still have a wonderful daughter?"

I could feel Mama's tears drip down my forehead, but it was okay if Mama cried this time. I felt my own tears starting. "I thought you forgot about me. That you didn't love me anymore."

"Never, Annie. I'd never stop loving you." Mama wiped her tears away and then laughed when she had to wipe my face, too. "I am stopping the medicine, though. At first it was good. It took away the sharpest edge of the grief, but then it made me numb to everything."

"I was sad, too, Mama. I miss the baby . . . Mary Kate . . . too. But it was like no one thought I had feelings. And no one would tell me what was happening."

"We didn't think you were old enough to understand, did we?" Mama hugged me even tighter. "Well, I can't promise to be happy again all at once, Annie. But I can be thankful for the family I do have, and so thankful to have Daddy coming back soon. Oh, I miss him."

"Me too."

"And I promise not to lock you out again. We need to be a family. If you have questions, we'll talk about it."

"Miss Eliza says the not knowing is the worst."

"Your Miss Eliza is very wise. Is she . . . ?"

Miss Eliza! I struggled to free myself from Mama's hug. I needed to find out about her. "Is Miss Eliza okay? She must have been stung, too. What if her throat swelled up?" I remembered seeing her standing all alone on the road, trying to catch her breath.

Mama got off the edge of the bed, but kept her hand on my shoulder. "I assume you're talking about the woman who brought you to us. Bobby told us something about her name . . . everything was so confusing. Anyway, Grandpa said he'd check on her this morning."

I took a deep breath. "She wouldn't want anyone checking on her. She didn't want any of the neighbors to know she was living there. Only Bobby and I were her friends."

"Where does she live, Annie?"

"In that little house. Right across from the road to Tater Hill."

Mama shook her head. "You have a whole life I know nothing about, don't you?"

By late afternoon the doctor said I could leave, and Grandpa came to pick us up from the hospital. When we got home, it was like I was the special guest, the way it was every time Daddy came home from his air force trips. First of all, Mama combed my hair the best she could and Grandma cut out the clumps of bee snarls. Then I soaked in the tub with baking soda dissolved in the water to calm the itching. When Grandma evened my hair up later, it curled under in a pageboy just below my chin. I liked the way it swung back and forth when I moved my head. Maybe I'd keep my hair shorter for now. I didn't like looking at myself in the mirror, though. My face was still puffy, and itchy red blotches from the bee stings covered my neck and arms. Just before Grandma swept up all the cut hair from the floor, I rescued one long lock for my journal scrapbook.

Grandpa shaved his beard off in celebration of my new haircut. It made him look younger. He put his waltz record on for us all to listen to while Grandma cooked a dinner of fried chicken and biscuits. All I wanted was water. I gulped down at least a gallon of it. But best of all was being at home like a family again. Even Bobby was there, and after his first surprised look at my short hair, he said he liked it. I was happy just to sit in my rocking chair and watch everything.

"The doctor said you'd feel tired and woozy for a few days. It's the antihistamine," Mama said after dinner was over. She held out a locket on a gold chain. "Grandma found this in her jewelry box. It's big enough to hold two pills. You'll have to wear it all the time, just in case you're ever stung again." When she fastened it around my neck, she added, "Even just one bee sting. You take the pills and go straight to the hospital."

"How am I supposed to get to the hospital if I can't drive?" I asked.

"Well, you know what I mean. You make sure someone takes you straight to a doctor or the hospital. I'll write a note to your teachers."

Just thinking about it made me shiver. I *never* wanted to go through anything like that again. A hundred stings or just one. How was I going to sleep tonight with visions of those bees swarming around in my head? I wasn't sure I'd even go into the woods or climb on any rocks ever again. But that meant not going back to the creek or . . .

"I have to go see Miss Eliza," I said. "Right now before it gets dark."

"That's nonsense," Grandma said. "Your grandpa and Bobby went down to check on the McGee . . . on her . . . this morning. She was fine."

"But I have to see her, Grandma, and tell her thank you."

"It's just not fitting for you to be down there in the home of a . . . an ex-criminal."

"She's not a criminal. Miss Eliza's a *good* person. She's my best friend in the whole world." I glanced over at Bobby and added, "Well, my best grown-up friend, anyway."

"She saved Annie, Mother." That was Mama speaking up, and I looked over at her in surprise. "She saved Annie's life, and we owe her everything."

Grandma nodded. "Well . . . you're right. But in that case, we should have her up here. That house is no more than a shack, not fit for anyone to live in or even visit."

"She won't come up here, Grandma. She won't go anywhere. Yesterday was the farthest away she's been from her house." I looked at Bobby, remembering what Miss Eliza had told us when we asked her why she always wore her bonnet. "It's her years of confinement. She doesn't like too much openness."

"Annie." Grandma shook her head. "You never cease to amaze me. What else do you know about this Miss Eliza McGee?"

I smiled. "She likes to read."

Chapter Twenty

Carrying a basket of leftover fried chicken, biscuits, two cucumbers, and snap beans from the garden, Bobby and Mama and I walked to Miss Eliza's house. Grandma had folded a little checked tablecloth in on top of the basket. "I've no table the right size for this, anyway," she said.

We stopped three times along the way. Mama still didn't have much energy for walking uphill, and even I was tired from all I'd been through. When we got to the little house, it didn't look so bedraggled. Of course the house itself still needed sprucing up, but the boards were off both front windows and the door had a fresh coat of paint, covering up those ugly red letters. The porch had been swept clean, and the green and gold woven rug hid the biggest cracks in the plank floor.

"Who did this?" I asked.

"Your grandpa and I did," Bobby said, trying to hide his smile. "First thing this morning, after we came to check on Miss Eliza and tell her you were going to be okay. We wanted to surprise you."

When Miss Eliza came to the front door, she said, "Oh lord, Annabel child, you are a sight for sore eyes." She ran her finger over the spots on my face, touched my short hair, and then hugged me tight.

"But what about you, Miss Eliza?" I asked. "Didn't you get stung, too?"

"Oh, some here and there, but those yellow jackets knew the hand that stirred their nest. They were after you, child."

Mama and Bobby had been standing back on the edge of the road, not quite on the porch. When Miss Eliza noticed Mama, she seemed suddenly shy again and reached a hand to her head as if trying to find the folds of her bonnet to hide behind, but her head was bare. Her hair hung loose in a long curtain down her back, as if it had been combed out to dry.

Mama handed the basket to Bobby and stepped onto the porch. She seemed shy, too, and didn't speak for a moment. "I have to thank you, Miss Eliza. For . . . for saving my Annie. And for being her friend."

"You're not beholden, Miz Winters. You have a fine girl here—the best there is."

"Yes, I know." Mama wrapped an arm around me. "My name is Maggie. Call me Maggie, please."

I broke the short silence that followed. "Miss Eliza, can I show Mama my weaving sampler?"

"Your weaving?" Mama asked, her eyes wide.

"I've been learning to weave," I said. "And both Bobby and I've been painting. The inside."

Mama shook her head. "You kids . . ."

With all four of us crowded into the tiny room, I sat on the bench in front of the loom, kicked my shoes off, and rested my toes on the treadles. It took a few minutes to find my place in the pattern. "Do I start with this treadle?"

"The second one," Miss Eliza answered. "Tighten your weft first. It's been sitting untouched."

After packing the weft into place several times with the beater bar, I stepped on the treadle and slid the shuttle across. Then I slammed the weft into place again, changed treadles, and slid the shuttle back, and so on. After a few minutes, I worked into a rhythm, slower than Miss Eliza, but still a step swoosh bang, step swoosh bang.

It was the kind of thing I could have gone on and on with forever, but Mama, Miss Eliza, and Bobby would have gotten tired of watching, and the light was getting dim. We had to be heading home before it was dark. I slammed the beater bar one more time and stopped. When I slid off the bench, I caught sight of my rock baby.

It was right where I had left it the last time I was here, nestled on top of the unused spools of yarn. *My rock baby.* Two days had passed since I had thought about it and even longer since I had held it. There was one more thing I needed to tell Mama.

I lifted the rock and cradled it against me. Yes, it still felt like a baby–the right weight, anyway–but it was solid and hard, unmoving. A baby would be soft and . . . well, moving or changing . . . *alive.* Yes, that was the word. And maybe I didn't need it now. The hole inside me wasn't so big and empty. . . . *But Mama might need it.*

"This is what I held, Mama. First when I was missing Mary Kate, and later when I was missing you." I handed it to her. "It's my rock baby," I whispered. "It helps to hold it."

At first Mama didn't know what to do with it. "Your rock baby?" she asked.

"Yes," I nodded. "Hold it like a baby."

Mama looked at me again with a question in her eyes, but she pulled the rock baby to her chest, and suddenly it slipped into the crook of her arm. She closed her eyes and swayed side to side. It was nearly a minute before I realized she was crying. She was trying to hold it in, but her whole body was shaking as if it were about to burst with tears and sobs.

Oh no, what have I done? "Mama, I'm sorry. I thought this would help." I put my arms around her. I thought maybe I should try to take the rock baby away, but no,

Mama was holding on to it so tight. She was bent over it now, as if trying to protect it, and she was crying out loud. Huge sobs that shook her entire body.

What have I done?

"It *is* helping her, child." Miss Eliza was taking charge now. "She needs to weep. Not cry, but weep, just as she is now." Miss Eliza eased Mama down onto the small cot along the wall and then she turned to Bobby and me. "Come. Let's go out. We'll let her be for a while. Your mama's grieving the baby girl she never got to hold."

We sat along the edge of the porch, since there was no furniture—so close to the road that our feet rested on the gravel. Bobby tossed stones out on the dirt, while we listened to Mama's weeping through the closed door. Two cars drove by, one too fast for me to recognize, but the second slowed down.

"That was the Coffeys," Bobby said. All four heads in the car turned to stare at us.

"Won't be long till the rest of Loggers Hollow knows I'm here," Miss Eliza said. "Gossip in the hills travels fast."

"I'm sorry, Miss Eliza," I said. "Everything's out in the open now, all because of me."

"No harm, child. It was time." Miss Eliza pointed across to the smaller, rutted road that wound steeply up the mountain. "I went up there, Annabel. Once I knew you were safe, I realized I'd left my house without once thinking about it, just to get you home."

"Did you go back to your old farm?" I asked.

"Yes, child. I took myself up that road to Tater Hill, right to the top. It was glorious and free, all those blue mountains fading away to pure sky. And my old home place—it's been kept right well, the fields plowed and planted. My daddy would be proud."

The last bit of pink sunset was slipping away above the trees when Grandpa came to get us in his station wagon. He said Grandma thought we were lost. Mama must have heard the car, because she appeared in the doorway at the same time, no longer crying but still holding the rock baby.

When we were settled in the car with the rock baby between us, Mama said, "You're a wise girl, Annie."

Chapter Twenty-one

Three days later, Daddy came home from Germany. He drove from Florida to pick us up. Mama and I knew he'd arrive sometime in the late afternoon, but it seemed to me that he'd never come. Finally Grandpa said, "Why don't you two just start walking down the road to meet him?"

So we did. We passed Loggers Hollow Church and the graveyard. Mama stood at the gate for a long time, but didn't go in. "We'll leave that till your daddy's here and the gravestone's in place," she said.

I pointed out the dam that Bobby and the Henderson boys had built in the creek. Then we passed the barn and next the Millers' house. There was no sign of Bobby. The only sound or sight was old Mr. Miller's tractor running out in one of the fields.

After that we started counting the hairpin curves, and it became a game. Which curve would we meet Daddy on? We finally came face to face with him on about the eighth one. Daddy looked so surprised to see us there. As soon as he pulled the car off the road and got out, he swung me up in the air and then hugged us both, but Mama the longest. In a way, it was kind of like the family hug at the end of *A Wrinkle in Time*.

When Daddy finally let go, he held my chin and looked at my face for a long time. Mama had told him over the phone about what had happened. "Those bees did a number on you, didn't they, Annie? And your new hairstyle—very chic." He hugged me again and tousled my hair before he turned back to Mama.

I knew they were trying to keep things happy, trying their best not to cry. "I thought you'd never come, Daddy. I didn't want to have to walk all the way back up the mountain." I said it to make him laugh. No one could ever think that was the only reason I wanted to see him.

"Well, I guess I could give you a ride to the house, if you insist," Daddy said. "Pile in."

I also knew Daddy wouldn't mind that I hadn't written

in my journal. I could show him all the little scraps and pieces of memories I had collected over the summer and tell him everything he needed to know in person.

And now it was time to go home to Florida, back to being a family together. But somehow it didn't seem quite right to leave. This was where Mary Kate would always be. She should have been going home with us. And of course there were Grandma and Grandpa, Bobby, and Miss Eliza to leave behind, too.

The car was packed, but we had one stop to make before we left. Mama had said she wouldn't go to the grave-yard until the gravestone was in place, and now there was no more putting it off.

I waited at the gate while Mama and Daddy walked ahead. I didn't want to be there when they saw the tiny grave. My own first sight of that little pile of dirt was still too hard a memory.

Grandma and Grandpa drove up in their station wagon with Miss Eliza in the backseat. It seemed Grandma and Miss Eliza were becoming friends—maybe not the kind who would tell each other secrets, but at least the kind who would share recipes and books and look out for each other. This way Miss Eliza wouldn't be so alone after I left.

Grandma carried a vase of white daisies, and Grandpa walked next to her with his hand on her elbow. Miss Eliza carried the Bible, and I carried my rock baby, memorizing its weight in my arms for the last time. Where was Bobby? He was supposed to be here, too.

I was the one who had planned this little funeral, if that was what it was. I had never been to a funeral before, so I wasn't sure, but maybe this was a little easier since the worst of the grief and tears had passed. Mary Kate deserved a funeral, something to show the world that she was loved and thought about and remembered. Even though we had never seen or held her, Mary Kate would always be a member of our family.

The grass was freshly mowed. Grandpa had taken care of that yesterday, and the good, clean smell of cut grass lifted my heart. Mary Kate's grave wasn't just a pile of dirt anymore. The grass had filled in around the edge, and the baby's breath fanned out across the top with its starry white blossoms. The gravestone was a soft granite gray, the color of Miss Eliza's eyes, and looked smaller than I thought it would, but also like it belonged there. Maybe it was okay that there wasn't a lamb carved into it.

We all stood silently in a half-circle around the grave until Grandma began with the Lord's Prayer and everyone joined in. Another silence, and then Grandpa said, "Annie, don't you have something you want to read?"

"Oh yes." Now that it was actually time, I felt nervous. First I laid my rock baby down at the foot of the grave, a place where I could always find it if Mama or I ever needed it again. Then Miss Eliza handed me the Bible with the verse from Isaiah already marked. If it was a good verse for Isaiah McGee, it was also a good verse for Mary Kate Winters.

I swallowed a few times before I found my voice. " 'He shall feed his flock like a shepherd. He shall gather the lambs with his arm, and carry them in his bosom, and gently lead those that are with young.' "

After that, we stood there for a few minutes with our heads bowed, thinking our own thoughts. Daddy had his arm tight around Mama, and I held her hand.

When we walked away, Miss Eliza started to sing. So quietly, at first I wasn't sure she *was* singing. After the first line, I recognized the strange, sad song that Miss Eliza had sung along with her hog fiddle. And it seemed just right.

> *"I'm just a poor wayfaring stranger,*
> *A-travelin' through this world of woe.*
> *But there's no sickness, toil, or danger*
> *In that bright world to which I go.*
> *I'm goin' there to see my father.*
> *I'm goin' there no more to roam.*
> *I'm just a-goin' over Jordan.*
> *I'm just a-goin' over home."*

And now it was time for good-byes. Everything had been dragged out so long, I thought it might be better if we just got in the car and drove away. There wasn't really anything else we could say.

But of course there were hugs for Grandma and Grandpa. "We'll be down to see you at Thanksgiving," Grandma said, trying to hide her handkerchief away in her pocket.

"If you want me to bring your rocking chair, Annie Annabel," Grandpa said, "just let me know."

"Thanks, Grandpa. But I think I want to keep it here in North Carolina for when I come back every summer." The yellow baby blanket and the tiny blue jacket were staying behind, too, tucked away in the drawer. It seemed right that they should stay close to Mary Kate and the rock baby. I *was* taking my weaving sampler of green cloth to hang on the wall above my bed at home, and I was wearing the watch that Daddy had brought me from Germany for my birthday gift.

Finally there was Miss Eliza, who looked so alone standing off by herself, as if she didn't belong in this family farewell. I hugged her, trying not to let any more tears start. "I'll write you letters," I promised. "Grandpa will get them to you."

"I'm not as good at writing as I am at reading, Annabel, but I reckon I'll try. Here's your book back, child." Miss Eliza handed me *A Wrinkle in Time.* "It's a fine book. I stayed up reading it by the light of my kerosene lamp. And you know ever' time I sing to my hog fiddle, I'll think of you."

I smiled, but couldn't say another word.

"Now you best get in your automobile with the rest of your family."

We were in the car now, and Daddy had the engine going, but I was still waiting for Bobby to come. "We need to leave, Annie."

"All right," I said, still watching out the window. And then I saw Bobby running up the road toward our car. I slid across the seat and rolled the window down.

"I was afraid you'd leave before I got here," Bobby said, out of breath.

"I know."

"Um." Bobby looked down at the road. "There's something I wanted to say to you. . . . Way back when we were in the barn that day . . . I didn't mean what I said . . . about getting over . . . well, about the baby."

"I know."

Those two words seemed to make a difference. "Good," Bobby said, and he smiled. "See you next year?"

"Yes, next year."

"Okay. We're off." Daddy pulled the car out onto the road and drove slow enough so we could all wave final good-byes to Bobby, Grandma, Grandpa, and Miss Eliza.

After the first curve, when everyone was out of sight, Daddy began to sing, the way he always did whenever we started off. It made our trips seem so exciting, as if there were all sorts of adventures waiting out there. . . .

"Off we go, into the wild blue yonder,
Climbing high, into the sun . . ."

I knew the exact curve in the road where I could turn around and look out the back window for my last view of Tater Hill. Daddy was done singing, and he and Mama were talking quietly up front. But I kept an eye out so I wouldn't miss it.

Yes, there it was, amidst the others. The one bare mountain with a rounded top, like a peeled potato. Tater Hill.

ACKNOWLEDGMENTS

My road to Tater Hill has been a long and winding one, with many drafts and welcome assistance from generous readers and teachers along the way. First, I'd like to thank and acknowledge those who established Spalding University's MFA program, where the first draft of *Road to Tater Hill* began as my creative thesis. I am proud to be a member of the program's second graduating class. Thanks also to my Spalding faculty mentors, authors in their own right: Lisa Jahn-Clough for her encouragement and feedback during my first semester, Louella Bryant for her focus on voice and for teaching me to use my "scientific" eye, and Susan Campbell Bartoletti for her lessons on structure and her faith in my story. Thank you, as well, to my many fellow MFA students who gave valuable comments during workshops.

On a technical level, my thanks go to Donna Hausermann, a Vermont weaver whom I met at the Shelburne Museum, and weaver Cindy Burkhart, both of whom lent me books and gave advice about the sounds and intricacies of the weaving process and warping (or preparing) the loom.

My heartfelt thanks go to my dear friends and fellow writers Teresa Crumpton and Patti Zelch, who have graciously read more drafts of *Road to Tater Hill* than I'd like to admit and who have each time given me constructive suggestions and encouragement. I am also indebted to my many other "writer" friends and readers: Gale Payne, Jackie Shields, Julie Mooney, Mary Bowman-Kruhm, Kathleen Thompson, Lois Szymanski, and Paula Zeller, as well as to my creative writing students, too numerous to name, but who faithfully attend my Misty Hill Lodge writing workshops and teach me as much as I teach them.

I was incredibly lucky to find an editor as supportive and discerning as Michelle Poploff. My thanks go to both Michelle and her assistant, Orly Henry, for urging me to dig deeper into my story.

Last, but certainly not least, there's my family, whose unflagging support of my writing dream made this book possible. Thank you to my daughter, Katie, and her husband, Douglas Fletcher; to my son, Daniel, and his wife, Mica; to my grandchildren, Connor (already a good reader and writer), Mairin, Annabel, and Aria; and espe-cially to my dear husband, Doug, for never being too busy to sit down and listen to me read my latest chapter aloud and to give honest feedback. I could not have done it with-out you. Finally, thank you to my devoted parents, whose own personal story was the seed for *Road to Tater Hill*.

EDITH M. HEMINGWAY, like her character Annie Winters, grew up in Florida and spent part of every summer at her grandparents' home in the North Carolina mountains. Blackberry picking on nearby Tater Hill was one of her favorite activities. When it was time for college, the North Carolina mountains drew her back. She earned her bachelor's degree at Appalachian State University in Boone. More recently, she completed her MFA in writing for children at Spalding University in Louisville, Kentucky. Edie now lives in Maryland with her husband in their 1930s log cabin, Misty Hill Lodge, nestled against the rocks of Chigger Hill. When she's not writing or teaching creative writing workshops, she enjoys kayaking with her family and learning to play the mountain dulcimer (or the hog fiddle, as Annie calls it). *Road to Tater Hill* is her first "solo" novel. You can read more about Edith M. Hemingway and her two co-authored Civil War novels at www.ediehemingway.com.